PREDILECTIONS

MARIANNE MOORE

Predilections

1955

THE VIKING PRESS · NEW YORK

Library of Congress catalog card number: 55-7376

PRINTED IN U.S.A. BY VAIL-BALLOU PRESS, INC.

CONTENTS

FOREWORD

SILENCE is more eloquent than speech—a truism; but sometimes something that someone has written excites one's admiration and one is tempted to write about it; if it is in a language other than one's own, perhaps to translate it—or try to; one feels that what holds one's attention might hold the attention of others. That is to say, there is a language of sensibility of which words can be the portrait— a magnetism, an ardor, a refusal to be false, to which the following pages attempt to testify.

M. C. M.

Autumn, 1954

PREDILECTIONS

FEELING AND PRECISION [1]

FEELING at its deepest—as we all have reason to know—tends to be inarticulate. If it does manage to be articulate, it is likely to seem overcondensed, so that the author is resisted as being enigmatic or disobliging or arrogant.

One of New York's more painstaking magazines asked me, at the suggestion of a contributor, to analyze my sentence structure, and my instinctive reply might have seemed dictatorial: you don't devise a rhythm, the rhythm is the person, and the sentence but a radiograph of personality. The following principles, however, are aids to composition by which I try, myself, to be guided: if a long sentence with dependent clauses seems obscure, one can break it into shorter units by imagining into what phrases it would fall as conversation; in the second place, expanded explanation tends to spoil the lion's leap—an awkwardness which is surely brought home to one in conversation; and in the third place, we must be as clear as our natural reticence allows us to be.

William Carlos Williams, commenting on his poem "The Red Wheelbarrow," said, "The rhythm though no more than a fragment, denotes a certain unquenchable exaltation"; and Wallace Stevens, referring to poetry under the metaphor of the lion, says, "It can kill a man." Yet the

[1] *Sewanee Review*, Autumn 1944.

lion's leap would be mitigated almost to harmlessness if the lion were clawless, so precision is both impact and exactitude, as with surgery; and also in music, the conductor's signal, as I am reminded by a friend, which "begins far back of the beat, so that you don't see when the down beat comes. To have started such a long distance ahead makes it possible to be exact. Whereas you can't be exact by being restrained." When writing with maximum impact, the writer seems under compulsion to set down an unbearable accuracy; and in connection with precision as we see it in metaphor, I think of Gerard Hopkins and his description of the dark center in the eye of a peacock feather as "the colour of the grape where the flag is turned back"; also his saying about some lambs he had seen frolicking in a field, "It was as though it was the ground that tossed them"; at all events, precision is a thing of the imagination; and it is a matter of diction, of diction that is virile because galvanized against inertia. In Louis Ginsberg's poem, "Command of the Dead," the final stanza reads:

> And so they live in all our works
>   And sinew us to victory.
> We see them when we most are gay;
>   We feel them when we most are free.

The natural order for the two mosts would be

> We see them when we are most gay;
>   We feel them when we are most free

but that would mean, being at our gayest makes us think of them, and being free makes us feel them—gross inaccuracy since these "mosts" are the essence of compassion.

"Fighting Faith Saves the World," an inadvertent ambiguity, as the title for a review of *Journey Among Warriors* by Eve Curie, seems to mean, fight faith and the world is saved; whereas to say, a fighting faith saves the world, would safeguard the meaning.

Explicitness being the enemy of brevity, an instance of difficult descriptive matter accurately presented is that passage in the Book of Daniel (X: 9, 10, 11) where the writer says: "Then was I in a deep sleep on my face, and my face toward the ground. And, behold, an hand touched me, which set me upon my knees and upon the palms of my hands. And I stood trembling." Think what *we* might have done with the problem if we had been asked to describe how someone was wakened and, gradually turning over, got up off the ground.

Instinctively we employ antithesis as an aid to precision, and in Arthur Waley's translation from the Chinese one notices the many paired meanings—"left and right"; "waking and sleeping"; "one embroiders with silk, an inch a day; of plain sewing one can do more than five feet." Anyone with contemporary pride thinks of W. H. Auden in connection with antithesis, as in *The Double Man* (the *New Year Letter*) he says of the devil:

> For, torn between conflicting needs,
> He's doomed to fail if he succeeds,
>
> .   .   .
>
> If love has been annihilated
> There's only hate left to be hated.

Nor can we forget Socrates' answer: "I would rather die having spoken in my manner than speak in your manner and live." And there is that very dainty instance of antithesis in Thomas Watson's and William Byrd's madrigal, "A Gratification unto Master John Case":

> Let Enuy barke against the starres,
> Let Folly sayle which way she please,
> with him I wish my dayes to spend, . . .
> whose quill hath stoode fayre Musickes frend,
> chief end to peace, chief port of ease.

When we think we don't like art it is because it is artificial art. "Mere technical display," as Plato says, "is a beastly noise"—in contrast with art, which is "a spiritual magnetism" or "fascination" or "conjuring of the soul."

Voltaire objected to those who said in enigmas what others had said naturally, and we agree; yet we must have the courage of our peculiarities. What would become of Ogden Nash, his benign vocabulary and fearless rhymes, if he wrote only in accordance with the principles set forth by our manuals of composition?

> I love the Baby Giant Panda,
> I'd welcome one to my veranda.
> I never worry, wondering maybe
> Whether it isn't Giant Baby;
> I leave such matters to the scientists—
> The Giant Baby—and Baby Giantists.
> I simply want a veranda, and a
> Giant Baby Giant Panda.

This, it seems to me, is not so far removed from George Wither's motto: "I grow and wither both together."

Feeling has departed from anything that has on it the touch of affectation, and William Rose Benét, in his preface to the *Collected Poems of Ford Madox Ford*, says: "Whether or not there is such a thing as poetic afflatus there are certain moments that must be seized upon, when more precise language than at any other time, is ready to hand for the expression of spontaneous feeling." My own fondness for the unaccented rhyme derives, I think, from an instinctive effort to ensure naturalness. "Even elate and fearsome rightness like Shakespeare's is only preserved from the offense of being 'poetic' by his well-nested effects of helpless naturalness." [2]

Chaucer and Henryson, it seems to me, are the perfection of naturalness in their apparently artless art of conveying emotion intact. In "Orpheus and Eurydice," Henryson tells how Tantalus stood in a flood that rose "aboif his chin"; yet

> quhen he gaipit thair wald no drop cum In;
>
> . . .
>
> Thus gat he nocht his thrist [to slake] no[r] mend.
>
> Befoir his face ane naple hang also,
> fast at his mowth upoun a twynid [threid],
> quhen he gaipit, It rollit to and fro,
> and fled, as it refusit him to feid.
> Quhen orpheus thus saw him suffir neid,
> he tuk his harp and fast on it can clink;
> The wattir stud, and tantalus gat a drink.

One notices the wholesomeness of the uncapitalized beginnings of lines, and the gusto of invention, with climax proceeding out of climax, which is the mark of feeling.

We call climax a device, but is it not the natural result of strong feeling? It is, moreover, a pyramid that can rest either on its point or on its base, witty anticlimax being one of Ludwig Bemelmans' best enticements, as when he says of the twelve little girls, in his story *Madeline*:

---

[2] Quoting myself, in *Contemporary Poetry*, Summer 1943.

They smiled at the good
and frowned at the bad
and sometimes they were very sad.

Intentional anticlimax as a department of surprise is a subject by itself; indeed, an art, "bearing," as Longinus says, "the stamp of vehement emotion like a ship before a veering wind," both as content and as sound; but especially as sound, in the use of which the poet becomes a kind of hypnotist—recalling Kenneth Burke's statement that "the hynotist has a way out and a way in."

Concealed rhyme and the interiorized climax usually please me better than the open rhyme and the insisted-on climax, and we can readily understand Dr. Johnson's objection to rigmarole, in his takeoff on the ballad:

I put my hat upon my head,
And went into the Strand,
And there I saw another man,
With his hat in his hand.

"Weak rhythm" of the kind that "enables an audience to foresee the ending and keep time with their feet," disapproved by Longinus, has its subtle opposite in E. E. Cummings' lines about Gravenstein apples—"wall" and "fall," "round," "sound," and "ground," worked into a hastening tempo:

But over a (see just
over this) wall
the red and the round
(they're Gravensteins) fall
with a kind of a blind
big sound on the ground

And the intensity of Henry Treece's "Prayer in Time of War" so shapes the lines that it scarcely occurs to one to notice whether they are rhymed or not:

> Black Angel, come you down! Oh Purge of God,
> By shroud of pestilence make pure the mind,
> Strike dead the running panther of desire
> That in despair the poem put on wings,
> That letting out the viper from the veins
> Man rock the mountain with his two bare hands!

With regard to unwarinesses that defeat precision, excess is the common substitute for energy. We have it in our semi-academic, too conscious adverbs—awfully, terribly, frightfully, infinitely, tremendously; in the word "stunning," the phrase "knows his Aristotle," or his Picasso, or whatever it may be; whereas we have a contrastingly energetic usefulness in John Crowe Ransom's term "particularistic," where he says T. S. Eliot "is the most particularistic critic that English poetry and English criticism have met with." Similarly with Dr. Johnson's "encomiastick," in the statement that Dryden's account of Shakespeare "may stand as a perpetual model of encomiastick criticism."

It is curious to see how we have ruined the word "fearful" as meaning full of fear. Thomas Nashe says of his compatriot Barnes—quoting Campion—"hee bragd when he was in France, he slue ten men, when (fearful cowbaby), he never heard a piece shot off but he fell on his face."

One recalls, as a pleasing antidote to jargon, Wyndham Lewis's magazine *The Tyro*, which defined a tyro as "an elementary person, an elemental usually known in journalism as the veriesttyro." "Very," when it doesn't mean true, is a word from which we are rightly estranged, though there

are times when it seems necessary to the illusion of conversation or to steady the rhythm; and a child's overstate-
ment of surprise upon receiving a gift—a playhouse—seems
valuable, like foreign-language idiom— "This is the most
glorious and terrific thing that ever came into this house";
but Sir Francis Bacon was probably right when he said,
"Hyperbole is comely only in love."

I have an objection to the word "and" as a connective
between adjectives—"he is a crude and intolerant thinker."
But note the use of "and" as an ornament in the sonnet
(66) in which Shakespeare is enumerating the many things
of which he is tired:

> And art made tongue-tied by authority,
> And folly (doctor-like) controlling skill,
> And simple truth miscall'd simplicity,
> And captive good attending captain ill.

Defending Plato against the charge of "allegorical bombast" in his eulogy of man's anatomy and the provision
whereby the heart "might throb against a yielding surface
and get no damage," Longinus asks, "Which is better, in
poetry and in prose, . . . grandeur with a few flaws or
mediocrity that is impeccable?" And unmistakably Ezra
Pound's instinct against preciosity is part of his instinct for
precision and accounts for his "freedom of motion" in saying what he has to say "like a bolt from a catapult"—not
that the catapult is to us invariably a messenger of comfort.
One of his best accuracies, it seems to me, is the word
"general" in the sentence in which he praises "the general
effect" of Ford Madox Ford's poem "On Heaven"—avoiding the temptation to be spuriously specific; and although
Henry James was probably so susceptible to emotion as to

be obliged to seem unemotional, it is a kind of painter's accuracy for Ezra Pound to say of him as a writer, "Emotions
to Henry James were more or less things that other people
had, that one didn't go into."

Fear of insufficiency is synonymous with insufficiency,
and fear of incorrectness makes for rigidity. Indeed, any
concern about how well one's work is going to be received
seems to mildew effectiveness. T. S. Eliot attributes Bishop
Andrewes' precision to "the pure motive," and the fact that
when he "takes a word and derives the world from it, . . .
he is wholly in his subject, unaware of anything else." Mr.
McBride, in the New York *Sun*, once said of Rembrandt
and his etching "The Three Crosses": "It was as though
Rembrandt was talking to himself, without any expectation that the print would be seen or understood by others.
He saw these things and so testified." This same rapt quality
we have in Bach's *Art of the Fugue*—his intensively private
soliloquizing continuity that ends, "Behold I Stand before
Thy Throne." We feel it in the titles of some of his works,
even in translation—"Behold from Heaven to Earth I
Come."

Professor Maritain, when lecturing on scholasticism and
immortality, spoke of those suffering in concentration
camps, "unseen by any star, unheard by any ear," and the
almost terrifying solicitude with which he spoke made one
know that belief is stronger even than the struggle to sur-
vive. And what he said so unconsciously was poetry. So
art is but an expression of our needs; is feeling, modified by
the writer's moral and technical insights.

HUMILITY, CONCENTRATION, AND GUSTO [1]

In times like these we are tempted to disregard anything that has not a direct bearing on freedom; or should I say, an obvious bearing, for what is more persuasive than poetry, though, as Robert Frost says, it works obliquely and delicately. Commander King-Hall, in his book *Total Victory*, is really saying that the pen is the sword when he says the object of war is to persuade the enemy to change his mind.

Three foremost aids to persuasion which occur to me are humility, concentration, and gusto. Our lack of humility, together with anxiety, has perhaps stood in the way of initial liking for Caesar's *Commentaries*, which now seem to me masterpieces. I was originally like the Hill School boy to whom I referred in one of my pieces of verse, who translated *summa diligentia* (with all speed): Caesar crossed the Alps on the top of a diligence.

In Caxton, humility seems to be a judicious modesty, which is rather different from humility. Nevertheless, could anything be more persuasive than the preface to his *Aeneid*, where he says: "Some desired me to use olde and homely termes . . . and some the most curyous termes that I could fynde. And thus between playn, rude and curyous, I stande

---

[1] Address, The Grolier Club, December 21, 1948.

abasshed"? Daniel Berkeley Updike has always seemed to me a phenomenon of eloquence because of the quiet objectiveness of his writing. And what he says of printing applies equally to poetry. It is true, is it not, that "style does not depend on decoration but on simplicity and proportion"? Nor can we dignify confusion by calling it baroque. Here, I may say, I am preaching to myself, since, when I am as complete as I like to be, I seem unable to get an effect plain enough.

We don't want war, but it does conduce to humility; as someone said in the foreword to an exhibition catalogue of his work, "With what shall the artist arm himself save with his humility?" Humility, indeed, is armor, for it realizes that it is impossible to be original, in the sense of doing something that has never been thought of before. Originality is in any case a by-product of sincerity; that is to say, of feeling that is honest and accordingly rejects anything that might cloud the impression, such as unnecessary commas, modifying clauses, or delayed predicates.

Concentration avoids adverbial intensives such as "definitely," "positively," or "absolutely." As for commas, nothing can be more stultifying than needlessly overaccented pauses. Defoe, speaking in so low a key that there is a fascination about the mere understatement, is one of the most persuasive of writers. For instance, in the passage about the pickpocket in *The Life of Colonel Jacque*, he has the Colonel say to the pickpocket: "Must we have it all? Must a man have none of it again, that lost it?" But persuasiveness has not died with Defoe; E. E. Cummings' "little man in a hurry" (254, *No Thanks*) has not a comma in it, but by the careful ordering of the words there is not an equivocal emphasis:

little man
(in a hurry
full of an
important worry)
halt stop forget relax

wait

And James Laughlin, the author of *Some Natural Things*, is eminent in this respect. His "Above the City" is an instance **of** inherent emphasis:

You know our office on the 18th
floor of the Salmon Tower looks
right out on the

Empire State & it just happened
we were finishing up some
late invoices on

a new book that Saturday morning
when a bomber roared through the
mist and crashed

flames poured from the windows
into the drifting clouds & sirens
screamed down in

the streets below it was unearthly
but you know the strangest thing
we realized that

none of us were much surprised because we'd always known that those
two Paragons of

progress sooner or later would per-
form before our eyes this demonstration of their
true relationship

Concentration—indispensable to persuasion—may feel to itself crystal clear, yet be through its very compression the opposite, and William Empson's attitude to ambiguity does not extenuate defeat. Graham Greene once said, in reviewing a play of Gorki's: "Confusion is really the plot. A meat-merchant and a miller are introduced, whom one never succeeds in identifying even in the end." I myself, however, would rather be told too little than too much. The question then arises, How obscure may one be? And I suppose one should not be consciously obscure at all. In any case, a poem is a concentrate and has, as W. H. Auden says, "an immediate meaning and a possible meaning; as in the line,

> a wedged hole ages in a bodkin's eye

where you have forever in microscopic space; and when George Herbert says,

> I gave to Hope a watch of mine,
> But he an anchor gave to me,

the watch suggests both the brevity of life and the longness of it; and an anchor makes you secure but holds you back."

I am prepossessed by the impassioned explicitness of the Federal Reserve Board of New York's letter regarding dangerous counterfeits, described by the Secret Service:

$20 FEDERAL RESERVE NOTE . . . faint crayon marks have been used to simulate genuine fibre. . . . In the Treasury Seal, magnification reveals that a green dot immediately under the center of the arm of the balance scales blends with the arm whereas it should be distinctly separate. Also, the left end of the right-hand scale pan extends beyond the point where the left chain touches the pan. In the genuine, the pan ends where it touches the chain. The serial numbers are thicker than the genuine, and the prefix letter "G" is sufficiently defective to be mistaken for a "C" at first glance, . . . the letters "ry" in "Secretary" are joined together. In "Treasury" there is a tiny black dot just above the first downstroke in the letter "u." The back of the note, although of good workmanship, is printed in a green much darker than that used for genuine currency.

December 13, 1948   Alfred M. Olsen, Cashier

I am tempted to dwell on the infectiousness of such matters, but shall return to verse. You remember, in Edward Lear's "The Owl and the Pussy-Cat," they said:

> "Dear Pig, are you willing to sell for a shilling
> Your ring?" Said the Piggy, "I will."

The word "Piggy" is altered from "Pig" to "Piggy" to fit the rhythm but is, even so, a virtue, as contributing gusto; and I never tire of Leigh Hunt's lines about the fighting lions: "A wind went with their paws." Continuing with cats, T. S. Eliot's account of "Mungojerrie and Rumpelteazer," "a very notorious couple of cats," is, like its companion pieces, a study in gusto throughout:

> If a tile or two came loose on the roof,
> Which presently ceased to be waterproof,
>
>   . . .
>
> Or after supper one of the girls
> Suddenly missed her Woolworth pearls:
> Then the family would say: "It's that horrible cat!
> It was Mungojerrie—or Rumpelteazer!"
> —And most of the time they left it at that.

The words "By you" constitute a yet more persuasive instance of gusto, in T. S. Eliot's tribute to Walter de la Mare upon Mr. de la Mare's seventy-fifth birthday:

When the nocturnal traveller can arouse
No sleeper by his call; or when by chance
An empty face peers from an empty house,

By whom: and by what means, was this designed?
The whispered incantation which allows
Free passage to the phantoms of the mind?

By you; by those deceptive cadences
Wherewith the common measure is refined;
By conscious art practiced with natural ease;

By the delicate invisible web you wove—
An inexplicable mystery of sound.

Dr. Maurice Bowra, pausing upon the query, Can we have poetry without emotion? seemed to think not; however, suggested that it is not overperverse to regard Cowper's "The Snail" as a thing of gusto although the poem has been dismissed as mere description:

Give but his horns the slightest touch,
His self-collective power is such,
He shrinks into his house with much
　　　Displeasure.

Where'er he dwells, he dwells alone.
Except himself, has chattels none,
Well satisfied to be his own
　　　Whole treasure.

Thus hermit-like his life he leads,
Nor partner of his banquet needs,
And if he meets one, only feeds
　　　The faster.

Who seeks him must be worse than blind,
He and his house are so combined,
If finding it, he fails to find
　　　Its master.

Together with the helpless sincerity which precipitates a poem, there is that domination of phrase referred to by Christopher Smart as "impression." "Impression," he says, "is the gift of Almighty God, by which genius is empowered to throw an emphasis upon a word in such wise that it cannot escape any reader of good sense." Gusto, in Smart, authorized as oddities what in someone else might seem effrontery; the line in Psalm 147, for instance, about Jehovah: "He deals the beasts their food."

> To everything that moves and lives,
> Foot, fin, or feather, meat He gives,
> He deals the beasts their food.

And in "A Song to David":

> Strong is the lion—like a coal
> His eyeball—like a bastion's mole,
> His chest against the foes:
>
> . . .
>
> But stronger still, in earth and air
> And in the sea, the man of pray'r,
> And far beneath the tide;
> And in the seat to faith assign'd
> Where ask is have, where seek is find,
> Where knock is open wide.

With regard to emphasis in Biblical speech, there is a curious unalterableness about the statement by the Apostle James: The flower "falleth and the grace of the fashion of it perisheth." Substitute, "the grace of its fashion perisheth," and overconscious correctness is weaker than the actual version, in which eloquence escapes grandiloquence by virtue of gusto.

Spenser is reprehended for coining words to suit the rhyme, but gusto in even the least felicitous of his defiances convicts the objecter of captiousness, I think, as in *The Shepheards Calender* (the "Chase After Love")—the part about "the swayne with spotted winges, like Peacocks trayne" —the impulsive intimacy of the word "pumie" substituted for a repetition of pumice stone brings the whole thing to life:

> I levelde againe
> And shott at him with might and maine,
> As thicke as it had hayled.
> So long I shott, that al was spent;
> Tho pumie stones I hastly hent
> And threwe; but nought availed:
> He was so wimble and so wight,
> From bough to bough he lepped light,
> And oft the pumies latched.

In any matter pertaining to writing, we should remember that major value outweighs minor defects, and have considerable patience with modifications of form, such as the embodied climax and subsiding last line. Wallace Stevens is particularly scrupulous against injuring an effect to make it fit a stated mode, and has

> . . . iceberg settings satirize

> .   .   .

> The demon that cannot be himself.

Beaumarchais, in saying, "A thing too silly to be said can be sung," was just being picturesque, but recordings of poetry convince one that naturalness is indispensable. One can, however, be careful that similar tones do not confuse the ear, such as "some" and "sun," "injustice" and the words "and justice"; the natural wording of uninhibited urgency, at its best, seeming really to write the poem in pauses, as in Walter de la Mare's lines about the beautiful lady, the epitaph:

> Here lies a most beautiful lady,
> Light of step and heart was she;
> I think she was the most beautiful lady
> That ever was in the West Country.

All of which is to say that gusto thrives on freedom, and freedom in art, as in life, is the result of a discipline imposed by ourselves. Moreover, any writer overwhelmingly honest about pleasing himself is almost sure to please others. You recall Ezra Pound's remark? "The great writer is always the plodder; it's the ephemeral writer that has to get on with the job." In a certain account by Padraic Colum of Irish storytelling, "Hindered characters," he remarked parenthetically, "seldom have mothers in Irish stories, but they all have grandmothers"—a statement borrowed by me for something I was about to write. The words have to come in just that order or they aren't pithy. Indeed, in Mr. Colum's telling of the story of Earl Gerald, gusto as objectified made the unbelievable doings of an enchanter excitingly circumstantial.

To summarize: Humility is an indispensable teacher, enabling concentration to heighten gusto. There are always objecters, but we must not be sensitive about not being liked or not being printed. David Low, the cartoonist, when carped at, said, "Ah, well—" But he has never compromised; he goes right on doing what idiosyncrasy tells him to do. The thing is to see the vision and not deny it; to care and admit that we do.

HENRY JAMES AS A CHARACTERISTIC AMERICAN [1]

To say that "the superlative American" and the characteristic American are not the same thing perhaps defrauds anticipation, yet one must admit that it is not in the accepted sense that Henry James was "big" and did things in a big way. But he possessed the instinct to amass and reiterate, and is the rediscerned Small Boy who had from the first seen Europe as a verification of what in its native surroundings his "supersensitive nostril" fitfully detected and liked. Often he is those elements in American life—as locality and as character—which he recurrently studied and to which he never tired of assigning a meaning.

Underlying any variant of Americanism in Henry James's work is the doctrine, embodied as advice to Christopher Newman, "Don't try to be anyone else"; if you triumph, "let it then be all you." The native Madame de Mauves says to Euphemia, "You seem to me so all of a piece that I am afraid that if I advise you, I shall spoil you," and Hawthorne was dear to Henry James because he "proved to what a use American matter could be put by an American hand. . . . An American could be an artist, one of the finest, without 'going outside' about it . . . ; quite, in fact, as if

[1] *Hound & Horn*, April: June, 1934.

Hawthorne had become one just by being American enough."

An air of rurality, as of Moses Primrose at the fair, struck Henry James in his compatriots, and a garment worn in his own childhood revealed "that we were somehow *queer*." Thackeray, he says, "though he laid on my shoulder the hand of benevolence, bent on my native costume the spectacles of wonder." On his return from Europe, James marveled at the hats men wore, but it is hard to be certain that the knowledge-seeking American in Europe is quite so unconsciously a bumpkin as Henry James depicts him. When Newman has said, "I began to earn my living when I was almost a baby," and Madame de Bellegarde says, "You began to earn your living in the cradle?" the retort, "Well, madam, I'm not absolutely convinced I *had* a cradle," savors of the connoisseur. Since, however, it is over-difficult for Henry James, in portrayals of us, not to be portraying himself, there is even in his rendering of the callow American a tightening of the consciousness that hampers his portrayal of immaturity.

"I am not a scoffer," the fellow-countryman says to Theobald, the American painter, and if it were a question either of being guarded or ridiculous, James would prefer to seem ridiculous. His respectful humility toward emotion is brave, and in diffidence, reserve, and strong feeling, he reminds one of Whittier, another literary bachelor whom the most ardent sadist has not been able to soil. We remember his sense of responsibility for the United States during the World War, and his saying of the Civil War, in *Notes of a Son and Brother*, "the drama of the War . . . had become a habit for us without ceasing to be a

strain. I am sure I thought more things under that head
. . . than I thought in all other connections together."
What is said in the same book of the death of Mary Temple,
the cousin who so greatly "had a sense for verity of character and play of life in others," is an instance of reverent,
and almost reverend, feeling that would defend him against
the charge of casualness in anything, if ever one were inclined to make it. It is not the artist, but responsibility for
living and for family, that wonders here about death and has
about "those we have seen beaten, this sense that it was
not for nothing they missed the ampler experience . . .
since dire as their defeat may have been, we don't see them
. . . at peace with victory." Things for Henry James glow,
flush, glimmer, vibrate, shine, hum, bristle, reverberate. Joy,
bliss, ecstasies, intoxication, a sense of trembling in every
limb, the heart-shaking first glimpse, a hanging on the pro-
longed silence of an editor; and as a child at Mr. Burton's
small theater in Chambers Street, his wondering, not if the
curtain would rise, but "if one could exist till then"; the
bonfires of his imagination, his pleasure in the "tender sea-
green" or "rustling rose-color" of a seriously best dress, are
too live to countenance his fear that he was giving us "an
inch of canvass and an acre of embroidery."

Idealism which was willing to make sacrifices for its self-
preservation was always an element in the conjuring wand
of Henry James. He felt about the later America "like one
who has seen a ghost in his safe old house." Of "Independence Hall . . . and its dignity not to be uttered, . . .
spreading staircase and long-drawn upper gallery, . . . one
of those rare precincts of the past against which the present
has kept beating in vain," he says, "nothing . . . would

induce me to revisit . . . the object I so fondly evoke." He would not risk disturbing his recollections of *The Wonder-Book* and *Tanglewood Tales* by rereading them, and Dickens "always remained better than the taste of over-hauling him." The aura is more than the thing. New Hampshire in September was "so *delicately* Arcadian, like . . . an old legend, an old love-story in fifteen volumes," and "Newport, . . . the dainty isle of Aquidneck," and "its perpetually embayed promontories of mossy rock," had "ingenuous old-time distinction . . . too latent and too modest for notation." Exasperated by the later superficiality of New York's determination "to blight the superstition of rest," he termed the public libraries "mast-heads on which spent birds sometimes alight in the expanses of ocean," and thought Washington Irving's Sunnyside, with its "deep, long lane, winding, embanked, overarched, such an old-world lane as one scarce ever meets in America, . . . easy for everything but rushing about and being rushed at." The "fatal and sacred" enjoyment of England "buried in the soil of our primary culture" leads him to regard London as "the great distributing heart of our traditional life"; to say of Oxford, "No other spot in Europe extorts from our barbarous hearts so passionate an admiration"; and for the two Americans in "hedgy Worcestershire" beneath an "English sky bursting into a storm of light or melting into a drizzle of silver, . . . nothing was wanting; the shaggy, mouse-colored donkey, nosing the turf, . . . the towering ploughman with his white smock-frock, puckered on chest and back." "We greeted these things," one says, "as children greet the loved pictures in a story-book, lost and mourned and found again . . . a gray, gray tower, a huge

black yew, a cluster of village graves, with crooked head-
stones. . . . My companion was overcome. . . . How it
makes a Sunday where it stands!"

Henry James's warmth is clearly of our doting native
variety. "Europe had been romantic years before, because
she was different from America," he said, "wherefore America would now be romantic because she was different from
Europe." His imagination had always included Europe; he
had not been estranged by travel nor changed by any "love-
philtre or fear-philtre" intenser than those he had received
in New York, Newport, or our American Cambridge. "Culture as I hold, is a matter of attitude quite as much as of
opportunity," he said in *Notes of a Son and Brother,* and
"one's supreme relation, as one had always put it, was one's
relation to one's country." In alluding to "our barbarous
hearts" he had, of course, no thought of being taken at his
word—any more than Mrs. Cleve did when abusing America—and even in the disillusions attendant upon return to
this country, he betrayed a parentally local satisfaction in
the way American girls dressed.

Nationally and internationally "the sensitive citizen," he
felt that patriotism was a matter of knowing a country by
getting the clue. Our understanding of human relations has
grown—more perhaps than we realize in the last twenty
years; and when Henry James disappoints us by retaining
the Northerner's feeling about the Confederate, we must
not make him directly contemporary, any more than we
dispute his spelling "peanut" with a hyphen. He had had no
contact with the South, and all the bother-taking Henry
James needed for doing justice to feeling was opportunity
to feel.

"Great things . . . have been done by solitary workers,"
he said, "but with double the pains they would have cost
if they had been produced in more genial circumstances."
Education for him, in a large sense, was conversation. Speaking of Cambridge, he said: "When the Norton woods,
nearby, massed themselves in scarlet and orange, and when
to penetrate and mount a stair and knock at a door, and,
enjoying response, then sink into a window-bench and in-
hale at once the vague golden November and the thick
suggestion of the room where nascent 'thought' had again
and again piped or wailed, was to taste as I had never done
before, the poetry of the prime initiation and of associated
growth."

We observe in the memoirs treasured American types:
"silent   Vanderpool, . . . incorruptibly   and   exquisitely
dumb," who "looked so as if he came from 'good people,'
. . . the very finest flower of shyness, . . . a true welter of
modesty, not a grain of it anything stiffer—"; "the ardent
and delicate and firm John May"—student at Harvard; and
there was Robert Temple, a cousin, "with a mind almost
elegantly impudent, . . . as if we had owed him to Thackeray"; and Mary Temple, " 'natural' to an effect of perfect felicity, . . . all straightness and charming tossed head,
with long light and yet almost sliding steps and a large
light postponing laugh." There was "a widowed grand-
mother who dispensed an hospitality seemingly as joyless as
it was certainly boundless," and Uncle Albert, a kinsman
who was " 'Mr.' to his own wife . . . his hair bristling up
almost in short-horn fashion at the sides," with "long,
slightly equine countenance, his eyebrows ever elevated as
in the curiosity of alarm."

A child is not a student of "history and custom, . . . manners and types"; but to say that Henry James as a child was "a-throb" with the instinct for meanings barely suggests the formidable paraphernalia which he was even then gathering. It is in "the waste of time, of passion, of curiosity, of contact—that true initiation resides," he said later; and no scene, strange accent, no adventure—experienced or vicarious—was irrelevant. When older, he alluded to "the maidenly letters" of Emerson; but in New York, Emerson had been strange and wonderful to the child he had invited "to draw near to him, off the hearth-rug." He was "an apparition sinuously and elegantly slim, . . . commanding a tone alien to any we heard round about"; and the schoolmate Louis De Coppet, in "his French treatment of certain of our native local names, Ohio and Iowa for instance, which he rendered . . . O-ee-oh and Ee-o-wah, . . . opened vitas." He said, "There hung about the Wards, to my sense, that atmosphere of apples and nuts . . . and jack-knives and 'squrruls,' of domestic Bible-reading and attendance at 'evening lecture,' of the fear of parental discipline and the cultivated art of dodging it, combined with great personal toughness and hardihood"; and there was " 'Stiffy' Norcom . . . whom we supposed gorgeous. . . . (Divided I was, I recall, between the dread and the glory of being so greeted, 'Well, Stiffy—!' as a penalty for the least attempt at personal adornment.)"

"You cannot make a man feel low," his Christopher Newman says, "unless you can make him feel base," and "a good conscience" is a pebble with which Henry James is extremely fond of arming his Davids. Longmore's "truth-telling eyes" are that in him which puzzled and tormented the Baron. "They judged him, they mocked him, they eluded him, they threatened him, they triumphed over him, they treated him as no pair of eyes had ever treated him." In every photograph of Henry James that we have, the thing that arrests one is a kind of terrible truthfulness. We feel also, in the letters and memoirs, that "almost indescribable naturalness" which seemed to him typical of his Albany relatives; a naturalness which disappears in the fancy writing of his imitators. If good-nature and reciprocity are American traits, Henry James was a characteristic American—too much one when he patiently suffered unsuitable persons to write to him, call on him, and give him their "work." Politeness in him was "more than a form of luxurious egotism" and was in keeping with the self-effacing determination to remain a devotee of devotees to George Eliot "for his own wanton joy," though unwittingly requested to "take away, please, away, away!" two books he had written. (Mrs. Greville had lent the books as introductory, previous to her calling with Henry James on the Leweses, but no connection was noticed between books and visitor.) The same ardor appears in the account of his meeting with Dickens. He speaks of "the extremely handsome face . . . which met my dumb homage with a straight inscrutability. . . . It hadn't been the least important that we should have shaken hands or exchanged platitudes. . . . It was as if I had carried off my strange treasure just exactly from under the merciless military eye—placed there on guard of the secret. All of which I recount for illustration of the force of action, unless I call it passion, that may reside in a single pulse of time."

Henry James belongs to "the race which has the credit of knowing best, at home and abroad, how to make itself comfortable," but there was in him an ascetic strain, which caused him to make Longmore think with disgust of the Baron's friend, who "filled the air with the odor of heliotrope"; and Eugene Pickering's American friend found "something painful in the spectacle of absolute inthralment, even to an excellent cause." Freedom, yes. The confidant, in comparing himself compassionately with the Eugene of their schooldays, says, "I could go out to play alone, I could button my jacket myself, and sit up till I was sleepy." Yet the I of the original had not "been exposed on breezy uplands under the she-wolf of competition," and there was not about him "the impertinent odor of trade." Some persons have grudged Henry James his freedom and have called it leisure; but as Theobald, the American painter, said of art, "If we work for her, we must often pause." Of *The Tragic Muse*, James said in a letter: "I took long and patient and careful trouble which no creature will recognize"; and we may declare of him as he did of John La Farge, "one was . . . never to have seen a subtler mind or a more generously wasteful passion, in other words a sincerer one." Reverting to the past of his own life, he was overpowered by "the personal image unextinct" and said, "It presents itself, I feel, beyond reason and yet if I turn from it the ease is less."

There was in him "the rapture of observation," but more unequivocally even than that, affection for family and country. "I was to live to go back with wonder and admiration," he says, "to the quantity of secreted thought in our daily medium, the quality of intellectual passion, the force

of cogitation and aspiration, as to the explanation both of
a thousand surface incoherences and a thousand felt felici-
ties." Family was the setting for his country, and the town
was all but synonymous with family; as would appear in
what is said of "the family-party smallness of old New York,
those happy limits that could make us all care . . . for the
same thing at once." It "is always a matter of winter twi-
light, firelight, lamplight." "We were surely all gentle and
generous together, floating in such a clean light social order,
sweetly proof against ennui." "The social scheme, as we knew
it, was, in its careless charity, worthy of the golden age . . .
the fruits dropped right upon the board to which we flocked
together, the least of us and the greatest"; "our parents
. . . never caring much for things we couldn't care for and
generally holding that what was good to them would be
also good for their children." A father is a safe symbol of
patriotism when one can remember him as "genially alert
and expert"—when "human fellowship" is "the expression
that was perhaps oftenest on his lips and his pen." "We
need never fear not to be good enough," Henry James says,
"if only we were social enough," and he recalls his mother
as so participatingly unremote that he can say, "I think we
almost contested her being separate enough to be proud of
us—it was too like our being proud of ourselves." Love is
the thing more written about than anything else, and in
the mistaken sense of greed. Henry James seems to have
been haunted by awareness that rapacity destroys what it is
successful in acquiring. He feels a need "to see the other
side as well as his own, to feel what his adversary feels"; to
be an American is not for him "just to glow belligerently
with one's country." Some complain of his transferred

citizenship as a loss; but when we consider the trend of his fiction and his uncomplacent denouements, we have no scruple about insisting that he was American; not if the American is, as he thought, "intrinsically and actively ample, . . . reaching westward, southward, anywhere, everywhere," with a mind "incapable of the shut door in any direction."

Conjuries That Endure [1]

FOR SOME of us, Wallace Stevens is America's chief conjurer—as bold a virtuoso and one with as cunning a rhetoric as we have produced. He has naturally in some quarters been rebuked for his skill; writers cannot excel at their work without being, like the dogs in *Coriolanus*, "as often beat for their barking/As therefore kept to do so." But like Handel in the patterned correspondences of the Sonata No. 1, he has not been rivaled:

> The body dies; the body's beauty lives.
> So evenings die, in their green going,
> A wave, interminably flowing.

His repercussive harmonics, set off by the small compass of the poem, "prove" mathematically, and suggest a linguist creating several languages within a single language. The plaster temporariness of subterfuge is, he says,

> Like a word in the mind that sticks at artichoke
> And remains inarticulate, . . .

[1] Review of Mr. Stevens' *Harmonium* (1923), *Ideas of Order* (1936), and *Owl's Clover* (1936), first printed in *Poetry*, February 1937; reprinted in *Literary Opinion in America*, edited with Introduction and Notes by Morton Dauwen Zabel (1937).

And besides the multiplying of "h's," a characteristically ironic use of scale should be noted, in "Bantams in Pine-Woods":

> Chieftain Iffucan of Azcan in caftan
> Of tan with henna hackles, halt!

The playfulness of such rhymings as "Scaramouche" and "barouche" is just right. But best of all, the bravura. Upon the general marine volume of statement is set a parachute-spinnaker of verbiage which looms out like half a cantaloupe and gives the body of the theme the air of a fabled argosy advancing.

Not infrequently Wallace Stevens' "noble accents and lucid, inescapable rhythms" point to the universal parent, Shakespeare. A novice of texts, if required to name author or century of the line, "These choirs of welcome choir for me farewell," might pay Wallace Stevens a high compliment; and the continuing of a word through several lines, as where we see the leaves

> Turning in the wind,
> Turning as the flames
> Turned in the fire,

is cousin to the pun of Elizabethan drama. We feel in the detached method of implication the influence of Plato, and an awareness, if not the influence, of T. S. Eliot. Better say each has influenced the other, with "Sunday Morning" and the Prufrock-like lines in "Le Monocle de Mon Oncle" in mind,

> Shall I uncrumple this much-crumpled thing?
>
> . . .
>
> For it has come that thus I greet the spring

and the Peter Quince-like rhythmic contour of T. S. Eliot's
"La Figlia che Piange." Each has an almost too acute concept of "the revenge of music," of a smiling, Voltaire-like,
self-directed pain, which, as John L. Sweeney says, "gores
itself on its own horns." Each is engaged in a similar, very
differently expressed search for that which will endure.

We are able here to see the salutary effect of insisting
that a piece of writing please the writer himself before it
pleases anyone else; and how a poet may be a wall of in-
corruptibleness against violating the essential aura of con-
tributory vagueness. Such heights of the romantic are
intimated by mere titles; one might hesitate to make trial
of the content lest it seem bathos; but Wallace Stevens is
a delicate apothecary of savors and precipitates, and no
hauteurs are violated. His method of hints and disguises
should have Mercury as consultant-magician, for in the
guise of "a dark rabbi," an ogre, a traveler, a comedian, an
old woman, he deceives us as the god misled the aged
couple in the myth.

To manner and harmonics is added an exultant grasp of
spectacle that is a veritable refuge of "blessed mornings,
meet for the young alligator"; an equivalence for jungle
beauty, arctic beauty, marine beauty, meridian, hothouse,
consciously urban or unconsciously natural beauty—which
might be alarming were it not for its persistent foil of dis-
satisfaction. This frugally unified opulence, epitomized by
the "green vine angering for life"—in Owl's Clover by the
thought of exploited Africa, "The Greenest Continent,"
where "memory moves on leopards' feet"—has been per-
fected stroke by stroke since the period of "the magenta
Judas-tree," "the indigo glass in the grass," "oceans in

obsidian," the white of "frogs," of "clays," and in "withered reeds"; until now, tropic pinks and yellows, avocado and Kuniyoshi cabouchon emerald-greens, the blent but violent excellence of ailanthus silk-moths and metallic breast-feathers—as open and unpretending as Rousseau's Snake-Charmer and Sleeping Gipsy—combine in an impression of incandescence like that of the night-blooming cereus.

Despite this awareness of the world of sense, one notices the frequent recurrence of the word "heaven." In each clime the author visits, and under each disguise, the dilemma of tested hope confronts him. In *Owl's Clover*, "the search for a tranquil belief" and the protest against the actualities of experience become a protest against the death of world hope; against the unorder of this "age of concentric mobs." Those who dare to forget that "As the man the state, not as the state the man," who divert "the dream of heaven from heaven to the future, as a god," are indeed the carnivorous owl with African greenness for its repast. The land of "ploughmen, peacocks, doves," of Leonardo da Vinci, has been "Combatting bushmen for a patch of gourds,/Loosing black slaves to make black infantry"; "the widow of Madrid/Weeps in Segovia"; in Moscow, in all Europe, "Always everything/That is is dead except what ought to be"; aeroplanes which counterfeit "the bee's drone" and have the powers of "the scorpion" are our "seraphim." Mr. Stevens' book is the sable requiem for all this. But requiem is not the word when anyone hates lust for power and ignorance of power as the author of this book does. So long as we are ashamed of the ironic feast, and of our marble victories—horses or men—which will break unless they are first broken by us, there is hope for the world. As R. P.

Blackmur has said, "The poems rise like a tide." They embody hope that in being frustrated becomes fortitude; and they prove to us that the testament to emotion is not volubility. Refusal to speak results here in an eloquence by which we are convinced that America has in Wallace Stevens at least one artist whom professionalism will never demolish.

There Is a War That Never Ends [1].

W ALLACE STEVENS protects himself so well against profanation that one does not instantly see the force of what he is saying, but with discernment focused the effect is startling; and it is a happy circumstance that we have *Notes toward a Supreme Fiction* not long after *Parts of a World*, for they are interrelated roots of the same tree.

Mr. Stevens has chosen "clouds" for "pedagogues." His "imagination's Latin"—compounded "of speech, paint, and music"—enables us to "see the sun again with an ignorant eye" as "A voluminous master folded in his fire," "Washed in the remotest cleanliness of a heaven/That has expelled us and our images." It is

> As if the waves at last were never broken,
> As if the language suddenly, with ease,
> Said things it had laboriously spoken.

[1] Review of Mr. Stevens' *Parts of a World* (1942) and *Notes toward a Supreme Fiction* (1942), in *Kenyon Review*, Winter 1943.

"Logos and logic . . ./And every latent double in the word," bring "the strong exhilaration/Of what we feel from what we think . . ./. . . a pure power." A poet does not speak language but meditates it, as the lion's power lies in his paws; he knows what it is "to have the ant of the self changed to an ox," "young ox," "lion," "stout dog," "bowlegged bear."

> It is a thing to have,
> A lion, an ox in his breast,
> To feel it breathing there,

to know that the "impossible possible" of imagination is so much stronger than reason that the part is equal to the whole. The poet—

> He is like a man
> In the body of a violent beast.
> Its muscles are his own . . .
>
> The lion sleeps in the sun.
> Its nose is on its paws.
> It can kill a man.

Delight "lies in flawed words and stubborn sounds," Mr. Stevens says; or, as the metaphoric ox apis might say, "bull words," "aphonies." "Words add to the senses . . ./Are the eye grown larger, more intense" and make fact what we want it to be. In this cosmos of reverie, a diamond is of poor worth as compared with the value to infinity of "words for the/Dazzle of mica," as gold was without value to the Incas but a delight to them because it was "the color of their revered Sun."

It is made evident, however, that imagination and the imaginer are different from images and imagers, from the nature-loving Narcissus who sees only himself in every pool, from "the strongly heightened effigy" which is but "a setting for geraniums." The eye of the imaginer is "the centre of a circle, spread/To the final full"; in it, "the part is the equal of the whole," "a self that touches all edges." And to this mind's eye in the circle, the holy health of the pines is derived from their color as much as from their resin.

> . . . the blue-green pines
> Deepen the feelings to inhuman depths.
>
> These are the forest. This health is holy,

Mr. Stevens says. Where he alludes to spruce trees and historic markers, we find that wording can be painting and that we are face to face with Maine's imperishable portrait: "everywhere spruce trees bury soldiers," and "Everywhere spruce trees bury spruce trees." The gulls "are flying/In light blue air over dark blue sea" that "flows/In sapphire, round the sun-bleached stones." Another major canvas is the one in *Notes toward a Supreme Fiction* about "a face of slate" with "vines around the throat":

> A lasting visage in a lasting bush,
> A face of stone in an unending red,
> Red-emerald, red-slitted-blue, a face of slate,
>
>   . . .
>
> Red-in-red repetitions never going
> Away, a little rusty, a little rouged
> A little roughened and ruder, a crown
>
> The eye could not escape, a red renown . . .
> Blowing itself upon the tedious ear.
> An effulgence faded, dull cornelian
>
> Too venerably used. . . .

"The elephant-colorings of tires," children "in pauvred colors," "the blue bushes," "the purple odor, the abundant bloom," the "red blue, red purple" lilacs that appear in these pages, are surely "paint."

Besides being speech and paint, the poems are music. Wallace Stevens is as susceptible to sound as objects were to Midas's golden touch. But he does not sophisticate his music. He listens to that of the bumblebee and the sea. Reverie is not a diplomatic occasion in Liberia. It must have "a music constant" like "the central humming of the sea." "It must give pleasure"—like "summer with its azure-doubled crimsons," like "The blue sun in his red cockade,

> Taller than any eye could see,
> Older than any man could be.

"Two things of opposite natures seem to depend on one another, the imagined on the real," Mr. Stevens says; we have "winter and spring," "morning and afternoon," "North and South," "sun and rain, a plural like two lovers."

Willingness to baffle the crass reader sometimes baffles the right one. That is to say, interrupted soliloquy can amount to disrupted logic. Yet delayed progression is wonderfully demonstrated here, as in the "profane parade": "a-rub, a rub-rub," "hip-hip," "hurrah, hip/Hip, hip, hurrah."

For the Connoisseur of Chaos, a "great disorder is an order"—"the eye, the ear, all things together," like "a repetition on one string." As for the "anti-master man" with "eye touched," "ear so magnified by thunder, parts, and all these things together were the truth"; so with Canon As-

pirin, "Beneath . . . the surface of/His eye and audible in
the mountain of/His ear, . . ." "It was not a choice

> Between, but of. He chose to include the things
> That in each other are included, the whole,
> The complicate, the amassing harmony.

This "anti-master man" seems to be a kind of supernatural
"skeleton" or "Nabob of bones" for whom

> . . . The cataracts
> As facts fall like rejuvenating rain,
> Fall down through nakedness to nakedness,
> To the auroral creature musing in the mind.

He feels that if one is to be "erudite in happiness," unnecessary learning must be left out—"anti-ideas and counter-
ideas," "reason's click-clack and its applied enflashings."
On arrival from Guatemala "at the Waldorf, . . . wild
country of the soul," he is again among "men remoter than
mountains." A now "chromatic florid Lady Lowzen in
glittering seven-colored changes," who had been "Flora
MacMort . . . in her ancestral hells, . . . skins the real
from the unreal." Whereas *eligo*—I choose—is "the moon
Blanche"; is truth, "the star, the vivid thing in the air that
never changes."

The "ancestral hells" have something in common with
James Joyce. Ezra Pound might, conceivably, address the
"Academy of Fine Ideas" as "My beards"; and life on the
battleship *Masculine*—"the captain drafted rules of the
world, Regulae mundi, as apprentice of Desartes"—puts
the stamp of its approval on certain Pound cantos. Like
Shakespeare and the aforementioned authors, Mr. Stevens

is not a prudish man, and since he feels that he is sufficiently restrained, perhaps we should allow comic relief to be offset by the larger meanings.

"To meditate the highest man . . . creates . . . what unisons create in music."

> . . .—Can we live on dry descriptions,
> Feel everything starving except the belly
> And nourish ourselves on crumbs of whimsy?

he asks. This highest man "is not a person" but "his breast is greatness." He is "the familiar man," the hero who "rejects false empire" and is "complete in himself despite the negations of existence." His affirming freedom of the mind is involved in "war that never ends." He and the soldier are one. Mr. Stevens has summarized it in *The Noble Rider and the Sound of Words*, where he says that "as a wave is a force and not the water of which it is composed, which is never the same, so nobility is a force. . . . It is a violence from within that protects us from a violence without. It is the imagination pressing back against the pressure of reality." In the final poem of *Notes toward a Supreme Fiction*, the violence from without is summarized—the soldier who is preserving that freedom of soul which gives rise to the violence within. Surely this is "the bread of faithful speech" for soldiers in the "war that never ends."

A Bold Virtuoso [1]

IN REVIEWING *Harmonium*—reprinted in 1931—Horace Gregory said, "All voices fall to a whisper and the expression of the face is indicated by a lifting of the eyebrow." [2] This is the perfect description of Wallace Stevens.

"Poetry is an unofficial view of being," Mr. Stevens says, and of our own today, "it wears a deliberately commonplace costume. . . . We do not write in the rhythm of *The Lady of the Lake*, any more than General Eisenhower would wear the armor of Agamemnon." Crispin

> . . . gripped more closely the essential prose
> As being, in a world so falsified,
> The one integrity for him, the one
> Discovery still possible to make,
> To which all poems were incident, unless
> That prose should wear a poem's guise at last.

The poet commits himself to that one integrity: antipathy to falsity. But "the imagination always makes use of the familiar," Mr. Stevens says, "to produce the unfamiliar," and "a deliberately commonplace costume" clothes themes far from commonplace, as we see in this metaphor of the shawl ("Final Soliloquy of the Interior Paramour"):

[1] From a series of commentaries on selected contemporary poets, Bryn Mawr, 1952.
[2] *New York Herald Tribune*, September 27, 1931.

Light the first light of evening, as in a room
In which we rest and, for small reason, think
The world imagined is the ultimate good.

.   .   .

Within a single thing, a single shawl
Wrapped tightly round us, since we are poor, a warmth,
A light, a power, the miraculous influence.

A single shawl—Imagination's—is wrapped tightly round
us since we are poor. Wallace Stevens embeds his secrets,
inventing disguises which assure him freedom to speak out;
and poverty is one of his favorites. In "Page from a Tale"
(*The Auroras of Autumn*), Hans is poor and chilly—Hans
"by his drift-fire" near "a steamer . . . foundered in the
ice," warmed by fires of his imagining; "a beggar in a bad
time" "opening the door of his mind" to the aurora borealis,
"to flames." "The scholar of one candle sees an arctic ef-
fulgence flaring on the frame of everything he is, and feels
afraid," but is at ease in "a shelter of the mind." "The stars
are putting on their glittering belts. They throw around
their shoulders cloaks that flash." Thus happiness of the
in-centric surmounts a poverty of the ex-centric. For poverty,
poetry substitutes a spiritual happiness in which the in-
tangible is more real than the visible and earth is innocent,
"not a guilty dream" but a "holiness," in which we are
awake as peacefully as if we lay asleep. One sees "new stars
. . . a foot across" come out; becomes someone ("In the
Element of Antagonisms")

On his gold horse striding, like a conjured beast,
Miraculous in its panache and swish.

Amid grandeurs of this sort, surrounded by the imagination's "mercies," one knows the difference between the

grand and the grandiose. With a metaphysician, an ogre, a grammarian, a nomad, an eel, as disguise for intensity, one is safe from "harangue," "ado," and the ambitious page.

Mr. Stevens carries to an extreme the art of understatement. Notice in the nun and the sunshade, i.e., "Certain Phenomena of Sound," Part III (*Transport to Summer*), the art of velvet emphasis, suspended till scarcely detectable:

> Eulalia, I lounged on the hospital porch,
> On the east, sister and nun, and opened wide
> A parasol, which I had found, against
> The sun. The interior of a parasol,
> Is a kind of blank in which one sees.
> So seeing, I beheld you walking, white,
> Gold-shined by sun, perceiving as I saw
> That of that light Eulalia was the name.
> Then I, Semiramide, dark-syllabled,
> Contrasting our two names, considered speech.

In Professor Gustave Cohen's *La Grande Clarté du Moyen-Age*, we have:

> Buona pulcella fu Eulalia
> Belle avret corps, bellezour anima.
> "Sage pucelle fut Eulalie
> Bel avait corps, mais plus belle avait l'âme."

Whereas for the nun on the hospital porch, personality is focused on speech. Names are part of Wallace Stevens' "persistent euphony"—a term used by William James in a letter to Henri Bergson, quoted by Wallace Stevens in "Figure of the Youth as Virile Poet." It is surely appropriate to "Le Monocle de Mon Oncle" (*Harmonium*):

A deep up-pouring from some saltier well
Within me, bursts the watery syllable.

The many water metaphors in the work of Wallace
Stevens are striking evidence, moreover, of his affinity—
say, synonymity—with rhythm. In "That Which Cannot
be Fixed" (*Transport to Summer*) he says:

>   . . . there is
>
> A beating and a beating in the centre of
> The sea, a strength that tumbles everywhere,

and in "This Solitude of Cataracts" (*The Auroras of
Autumn*), the river "kept flowing and never the same way
twice, flowing/Through many places, as if it stood still in
one"—a master-description of the uniformity in variety of
flowing water. We find unrhymed lines that have the effect
of rhyme:

> blue as of a secret place
> in the anonymous color of the universe;

but even without rhyme, Mr. Stevens is a master of sound,
as in "the icy Elysée"; "a sovereign, a souvenir, a sign"; "the
fidgits of a fire"; "from finikins to find finikin, edgings and
inchings of final form." We have "shawl" and "shell,"
"swell" and "shawl"; and "hill" and "sail"—in "Continual
Conversation with a Silent Man" (*Transport to Summer*):

> The broken cartwheel on the hill.

> As if, in the presence of the sea,
> We dried our nets and mended sail.

The compacted spontaneity with pauses, counterpoint,
and euphony of "Certain Phenomena of Sound"—already
quoted—match La Fontaine: ". . . sister and nun," I

"opened wide/A parasol, which I had found, against/The sun."

Together with the infallible mastery of pause and tone, there is in Wallace Stevens a certain demureness of statement, as when—setting down what he has to say with the neatest kind of precision—he says, "the poet mumbles"; much as La Fontaine affects impartiality, ponders the practice of predecessors, and submits preference to "the authorities"; or says of Cupid blinded by Folly, "but perhaps a service was done./Let lovers say; a lonely man has no criterion." Surely the term that Pierre Schneider applies to La Fontaine applies to Wallace Stevens, "a melomane." In his treatise "Le Paradis et l'Habitant," Mr. Schneider says of La Fontaine, his "speech is a golden thread of words" leading us into gardens of Versailles where the grass is soft and thick and the waters against walls of green "are lost in a crystal geometry that never ends." "His prose is not less poetic than his poetry," Mr. Schneider says. The same may be said of Wallace Stevens' essay, "Figure of the Youth as Virile Poet," where he speaks of a place in which it would be pleasant to spend a holiday, where he imagines "a rock that sparkles, a blue sea that lashes, and hemlocks in which the sun can merely fumble."

.t Is Not Forbidden to Think" [1]

Collected Poems of T. S. Eliot, complete except for *Murder in the Cathedral*, are chronological through 1930, and two tendencies mark them all: the instinct for order and a "contempt for sham." "I am not sure," Mr. Eliot says in "The Uses of Poetry," "that we can judge and enjoy a man's poetry while leaving wholly out of account all the things for which he cared deeply, and on behalf of which he turned his poetry to account." He detests a conscience, a politics, a rhetoric, that is neither one thing nor the other. For him hell is hell in its awareness of heaven; good is good in its distinctness from evil; precision is precision as triumphing over vagueness. In *The Rock* he says, "Our age is an age of moderate virtue/And of moderate vice." Among Peter the Hermit's "hearers were a few good men,/Many who were evil,/And most who were neither."

Although, as a critic, Mr. Eliot manifests at times an almost combative sincerity, by doing his fighting in prose he is perhaps the more free to do his feeling in verse. But in his verse, judgment indeed remains awake. His inability to

[1] Review of T. S. Eliot's *Collected Poems* (1936) in *The Nation*, May 27, 1936.

elude "the Demon of Thought" appears in Prufrock's decision:

> Oh, do not ask, "What is it?"
> Let us go and make our visit.

and in the self-satire of "Lines for Cuscuscaraway and Mirza Murad Ali Beg":

> How unpleasant to meet Mr. Eliot!
> With his features of clerical cut,
>
> . . .
>
> And his conversation, so nicely
> Restricted to What Precisely
> And If and Perhaps and But.

One sees in this collected work, conscience—directed toward "things that other people have desired," asking, "are these things right or wrong"—and an art which from the beginning has tended toward drama. We have in *The Waste Land* a stage for a fortune-teller, for a game of chess, for a sermon, for music of various kinds, for death by drowning and death from thirst; finally for a boat responding gaily "to the hand, expert with sail and oar," and for a premonition of Peace. "T. S. Eliot forged the first link between . . . psychological and historical discoveries of his period and his period's poetry," Louise Bogan says; "far from being a poem of despair," *The Waste Land* "projects a picture of mankind at its highest point of ascetic control —St. Augustine, Buddha—as well as mankind at its lowest point of spiritual stupor, ignorance, and squalor."

In *Ash Wednesday* and later, Mr. Eliot is not warily considering "matters that with myself I too much discuss/Too

much explain"; he is *in* them, and *Ash Wednesday* is perhaps the poem of the book—a summit, both as content, in
its unself-justifying humility, and technically, in the lengthened phrase and gathered force of enmeshed rhymes.

Mr. Eliot's aptitude for mythology and theology sometimes pays us the compliment of expecting our reading to
be more thorough than it is; but correspondences of allusion
provide an unmistakable logic of preference: for stillness,
intellectual beauty, spiritual exaltation, the white dress,
"the glory of the humming-bird," childhood, and wholeness
of personality—in contrast with noise, evasiveness, aimlessness, fog, scattered bones, broken pride, rats, draughts under
the door, distortion, "the stye of contentment." Horror,
which is unbelief, is the opposite of ecstasy; and wholeness,
which is the condition of ecstasy, is to be "accepted and
accepting." That is to say, we are of a world in which light
and darkness, "appearance and reality," "is and seem," are
includable alternatives.

Words of special meaning recur with the force of a
theme: "hidden," "the pattern," and "form." Fire, the
devourer, is a purifier; and as God's light is for man, the
sun is life for the natural world. Concepts and images are
toothed together so that one poem rests on another and is
part of what came earlier; the musical theme at times being
separated by a stanza as the argument sometimes is continued from the preceding poem—"O hidden" in "Difficulties of a Statesman" completing the "O hidden" in
"Triumphal March."

The period including *Ash Wednesday*, concerned with
"The infirm glory of the positive hour," is succeeded by the
affirmative one to which *Murder in the Cathedral* belongs,

and "Burnt Norton" ("And do not call it fixity," "The detail of the pattern is movement.") :

> We move above the moving tree
> In light upon the figured leaf
> And hear upon the sodden floor
> Below, the boarhound and the boar
> Pursue their pattern as before
> But reconciled among the stars.

In "Usk," Mr. Eliot depicts the *via media* of self-discipline:

> Where the roads dip and where the roads rise
> Seek only there
> Where the gray light meets the green air
> The hermit's chapel, the pilgrim's prayer.

One notices here the compacting of visible, invisible, indoors, and outdoors; and that in these later poems statement becomes simpler, the rhythm more complex.

Mr. Eliot has tried "to write poetry which should be essentially poetry, with nothing poetic about it, poetry standing naked in its bare bones, or . . . so transparent that in reading it we are intent on what the poem *points at* and not on the poetry." He has not evaded "the deepest terrors and desires," depths of "degradation," and heights of "exaltation," or disguised the fact that he has "walked in hell" and "been rapt to heaven."

Those who have power to renounce life are those who have it; one who attains equilibrium in spite of opposition to himself from within, is stronger than if there had been no opposition to overcome; and in art, freedom evolving from a liberated constraint is more significant than if it had not by nature been cramped. Skepticism, also constraint, are part of Mr. Eliot's temperament. Art, however, if concealing the artist, exhibits his "angel"; like the unanticipated florescence of fireworks as they expand with the felicitous momentum of "unbroke horses"; and this effect of power we have in "Cape Ann"—denominated a minor poem:

> O quick quick quick, quick hear the song-sparrow,
> Swamp-sparrow, fox-sparrow, vesper-sparrow
> At dawn and dusk. . . .

Another unemphasized triumph of tempo and terseness, we have in "Lines for an Old Man":

> The tiger in the tiger-pit
> Is not more irritable than I.
> The whipping tail is not more still
> Than when I smell the enemy
> Writhing in the essential blood
> Or dangling from the friendly tree.
> When I lay bare the tooth of wit
> The hissing over the archèd tongue
> Is more affectionate than hate,
> More bitter than the love of youth,
> And inaccessible by the young.
> Reflected from my golden eye
> The dullard knows that he is mad.
> Tell me if I am not glad!

In the above lines we have an effect—have we not?—of order without pedantry, and of terseness that is synonymous with a hatred of sham.

Reticent Candor [1]

THAT T. S. Eliot and Wallace Stevens have certain qualities in common perhaps is obvious—in reticent candor and emphasis by understatement. Speaking as from ambush, they mistrust rhetoric—taking T. S. Eliot's definition of the word, in his "Rhetoric and Poetic Drama," as "any adornment or inflation of speech which is not used for a particular effect but for general impressiveness." Of "omnivorous perspicacity," [2] each has been concerned from the first with the art and use of poetry, and has continued to be a poet. And although too much importance should not be attached to this, the following passages are of interest, it seems to me, as revealing consanguinities of taste and rhythm; in T. S. Eliot's "La Figlia che Piange":

> So I would have had him leave,
> So I would have had her stand and grieve,

and Wallace Stevens' "Peter Quince at the Clavier":

> So evenings die, in their green going,
> A wave, interminably flowing.

> . . .

> So maidens die, to the auroral
> Celebration of a maiden's choral.

[1] From a series of commentaries on selected contemporary poets, Bryn Mawr, 1952.
[2] Hugh Kenner in another connection (*Hudson Review*, Autumn 1949).

Reviewing *The Waste Land*, Conrad Aiken said, "T. S. Eliot's net is wide and the meshes are small . . ."; [3] especially wide and small as prose bearing on poetry. In "The Music of Poetry," Mr. Eliot says, "Poetry must give pleasure"; [4] "find the possibilities of your own idiom"; "poetry must not stray too far from the ordinary language we use and hear"—principles in keeping with the following statements quoted by Mr. Eliot from W. P. Kerr: "the end of scholarship is understanding," and "the end of understanding is enjoyment," "enjoyment disciplined by taste."

T. S. Eliot's concern with language has been evident all along—as when he says in "A Talk on Dante," "The whole study and practice of Dante seems to me, to teach that the poet should be the servant of his language, rather than the master of it." And "To pass on to posterity one's own language, more highly developed, more refined, and more

[3] *New Republic*, February 7, 1923.

[4] During World War II, George Dillon was stationed in Paris and, writing to *Poetry* (issue of October 1945), said: "The other night I went to hear T. S. Eliot's lecture on the poet's role in society. . . . The little Salle des Centraux in the rue Jean-Goujon (Champs-Elysées neighborhood) . . . was packed with the most miscellaneous gathering. . . . Finally Paul Valéry stepped to the platform. . . . After Valéry's introduction, Eliot stood to acknowledge the applause, then sat down, in French fashion, to give his talk. . . . He made a few remarks in English, expressing his emotion at being once more, and at such a time, in Paris. . . . Then . . . he read his lecture in French—I was interested to note, with an almost perfect French *rhythm*. His lecture elaborated the distinction between the apparent role and the true role of the poet, stressing the idea that *a writer who is read by a small number* over a long period may have a more important social function than one who enjoys great popularity over a limited period; also, that the people who do not even know the names of their great national poets are not the less profoundly influenced by what they have written. . . . He emphasized his belief that poetry must give pleasure or it cannot do good. Good poetry is that which is '*capable de donner du plaisir aux honnêtes gens.*' The part of his lecture which the French seemed to enjoy most was his definition of the two kinds of bad poet—the '*faux mauvais,*' those who have a spurt of writing poetry in their youth, and the '*vrais mauvais,*' those who keep on writing it."

precise than it was before one wrote it, that is the highest achievement of the poet as poet. . . . Dante seems to me," he says, "to have a place in Italian literature which in this respect, only Shakespeare has in ours. They gave body to the soul of the language, conforming themselves to what they deemed its possibilities." Furthermore, "In developing the language, enriching the meaning of words and showing how much words can do," Mr. Eliot says, the poet "is making possible a much greater range of emotion and perception for other men because he gives them the speech in which more can be expressed." Then, "The kind of debt that I owe to Dante is the kind that goes on accumulating. . . . Of Jules La Forgue, for instance, I can say that he was the first . . . to teach me the poetic possibilities of my own idiom of speech. . . . I think that from Baudelaire I learned first, a precedent for the poetical possibilities, never developed by any poet writing in my own language, of the more sordid aspects of the modern metropolis, of the possibility of fusion between the sordidly realistic and the phantasmagoric, the possibility of the juxtaposition of the matter-of-fact and the fantastic . . . and that the source of new poetry might be found in what had been regarded [as] the intractably unpoetic. . . . One has other debts, innumerable debts," he says, "to poets of another kind. . . . There are those who remain in one's mind as having set the standard for a particular poetic virtue, as Villon for honesty, and Sappho for having fixed a particular emotion in the right and the minimum number of words" [5]—the words "poetic" and "minimum" carefully not omitted, one notices.

[5] *Kenyon Review*, Spring 1952.

To quote what is in print seems unnecessary, and manner is scarcely a subject for commentary; yet something is to be learned, I think, from a reticent candor in which openness tempts participation, besides placing experience at our service—as in the above-mentioned commentary, "A Talk on Dante"; as in "Poetry and Drama" (the Theodore Spencer Memorial Lecture); and in the retrospect of Ezra Pound that appeared in the September 1946 issue, of *Poetry*.

In "Poetry and Drama," conversationally confidential again, Mr. Eliot asks if poetic drama has anything potentially to offer that prose can not. "No play should be written in verse," he says, "for which prose is dramatically adequate." "The audience should be too intent upon the play to be wholly conscious of the medium," and "the difference is not so great as we might think between prose and verse." "Prose on the stage," he says, "is as artificial as verse," the reason for using verse being that "even the pedestrian parts of a verse play have an effect upon the hearers without their being conscious of it." "If you were hearing *Hamlet* for the first time," Mr. Eliot says, "without knowing anything about the play, I do not think it would occur to you to ask whether the speakers were speaking in verse or prose." For example, the opening lines:

> Bernardo: Who's there?
> Francisco: Nay, answer me: stand and unfold yourself.
> Bernardo: Long live the king!
>
> .   .   .
>
> Francisco: Not a mouse stirring.
> Bernardo: Well, good night.[6]

[6] Lindsay Anderson says of Marcel Pagnol's *Amlé*, performed in the courtyard of the thirteenth-century Château of the Roi René at Anger:

Then of his own "intentions, failures and partial success,"
Mr. Eliot says that "*Murder in the Cathedral* was produced
for an audience of those serious people who go to 'festivals'
and expect to have to put up with poetry—though some
were not quite prepared for what they got." "The style," he
says, "had to be neutral, commited neither to the present
nor to the past. As for the versification . . . what I kept in
mind was the versification of *Everyman*"; despite its only
"negative merit in my opinion," it "succeeded in avoiding
what had to be avoided. . . . What I should hope might
be achieved is that the audience should find . . . that it is
saying to itself: 'I could talk in poetry too!' " "I was determined in my next play," he says, "to take the theme of
contemporary life. *The Family Reunion* was the result.
Here my first concern was . . . to find a rhythm in which
the stresses could be made to come where we should naturally put them. . . . What I worked out is substantially
what I have continued to employ: a line of varying length
and varying number of syllables, with a caesura and three
stresses. The caesura and the stresses may come at different
places . . . the only rule being that there must be one stress
on one side of the caesura and two on the other. . . . I
soon saw that I had given my attention to versification at
the expense of plot and character." Then the Furies. "We
put them on the stage. They looked like uninvited guests
from a fancy-dress ball. . . . We concealed them behind
gauze. We made them dimmer, and they looked like shrub-

"The outstanding virtue of Pagnol's translation (never played before) is its
directness, its lucidity, its consistent sense of the dramatic. . . . Warmer,
more vital than Gide, the author of *Marius* has given his version [of *Hamlet*]
the impact of contemporary theatrical speech. . . . In its new language, the
lyric drama seems to reveal its contours afresh" (*The Observer,* July 4,
1954).

bery just outside the window"; diagnosis followed in the
same vein of candor, by, "My hero now strikes me as an un-
sufferable prig." Next: "You will understand . . . some of
the errors that I endeavored to avoid in designing *The Cock-
tail Party*. To begin with, no chorus, and no ghosts. . . . As
for the verse, I laid down for myself the ascetic rule to avoid
poetry which could not stand the test of dramatic utility:
with such success, indeed, that it is perhaps an open question
whether there is any poetry in the play at all." Then, as flatly
objective, "I am aware that the last act of my play only just
escapes, if indeed it does escape, the accusation of being not
a last act but an epilogue." "I have, I believe," he says in
conclusion, "been animated by a better motive than egoism.
I have wished to put on record for what it may be worth to
others, some account of the difficulties I have encountered
and the weaknesses I have had to overcome, and the mistakes into which I have fallen." Now this kind of candor
seems to me not short of sensational—as technical exposition to which carefully accurate informality lends persuasiveness.

The retrospect of Ezra Pound's London years shares the
(to me, useful) tone of the Spencer lecture; I detect no
difference between it and conversation. Mr. Eliot is speaking here of 1908 and of Ezra Pound as suggesting "a usable
contemporary form of speech at a time of stagnation." He
says, "Browning was more of a hindrance than a help for
he had gone some way, but not far enough in discovering a
contemporary idiom. . . . The question was still: where
do we go from Swinburne? and the answer appeared to be,
nowhere." One notes the adjectives, numerous without
heaviness: "Pound was then living in a small dark flat in

Kensington. In the largest room he cooked, by artificial light; in the lightest but smallest room, which was inconveniently triangular, he did his work and received his visitors. [He gave the impression of being transient,] due, not only to his restless energy—in which it was difficult to distinguish the energy from the restlessness and fidgits . . . but to a kind of resistance against growing into any environment. . . . For a time, he found London, and then Paris, the best center for his attempts to revitalize poetry. But though young English writers, and young writers of any nationality, could count on his support if they excited his interest, the future of American letters was what concerned him most."

"No poet, furthermore was, without self-depreciation, more unassuming about his own achievement in poetry," Mr. Eliot says. "The arrogance which some people have found in him is really something else. . . . [He] would go to any lengths of generosity and kindness; from inviting constantly to dinner, a struggling author whom he suspected of being under-fed, or giving away clothing (though his shoes and underwear were almost the only garments which resembled those of other men sufficiently to be worn by them), to trying to find jobs, collect subsidies, get work published and then get it criticized and praised."

Pound's critical writing, Mr. Eliot goes on to say, "forms a corpus of poetic doctrine. . . . The opinion has been voiced that Pound's reputation will rest upon his criticism and not upon his poetry. I disagree. It is on his total work for literature that he must be judged: on his poetry, *and* his criticism, *and* his influence at a turning point in literature. In any case, his criticism takes its signficance from the fact

that it is the writing of a poet about poetry; it must be read
in the light of his own poetry, as well as of poetry by other
men whom he championed. . . . You cannot wholly understand Aristotle's doctrine of tragedy without reference
to the remains of the Attic drama upon which Aristotle's
generalizations are founded." And, bearing upon this, Mr.
Eliot quotes Ezra Pound as saying that "theoretically criticism tries to . . . serve as a gunsight, but that the man
who formulates any forward reach of co-ordinating principle is the man who produces the demonstration. . . .
They proceed as two feet of one biped."

"I know that one of the temptations against which I have
to be on guard," Mr. Eliot says, "is trying to re-write somebody's poem in the way in which I should have written it
myself. Pound never did that: he tried first to understand
what one was attempting to do, and then tried to help one
do it in one's own way." As part of the definiteness with
openness which aids this commentary, we have the following aside: "In the Cantos there is an increasing defect of
communication. . . . I am incidentally annoyed, myself,
by occasional use of the peculiar orthography which char-
acterizes Pound's correspondence and by lines written in
what he supposes to be Yankee dialect. But the craftsman
up to this moment . . . has never failed." (One notices
"moment" as replacing the usual, less intent word "time.")

"Pound's 'erudition,' " Mr. Eliot says, "has been both
exaggerated and . . . under-estimated: for it has been
judged chiefly by scholars who did not understand poetry,
and by poets who have had little scholarship." (Apropos
here, Dr. Tenney Frank's statement to students at Bryn
Mawr in connection with Ezra Pound's "Homage to Sextus

Propertius": anyone might render a line impeccably; few can communicate appetite for the thing and present content with the brio with which Ezra Pound presents it.)

"Pound's great contribution to the work of other poets," Mr. Eliot says, "is his insistence upon the immensity of the amount of *conscious* labor to be performed by the poet; and his invaluable suggestions for the kind of training the poet should give himself—study of form, metric and vocabulary in the poetry of divers literature, and study of good prose. . . . He also provides an example of devotion to 'the art of poetry' which I can only parallel in our time by the example of Valéry, and to some extent that of Yeats: and to mention these names is to give some impression of Pound's importance as an exponent of the art of poetry" at a time when

> The "age demanded" chiefly a mould in plaster,
> Made with no loss of time,
> A prose kinema, not, not assuredly, alabaster
> Or the "sculpture" of rhyme.

As Ezra Pound, J. V. Healy says, followed T. E. Hulme's precept, that language "should endeavor to arrest you, and to make you continuously see a physical thing, and prevent your gliding through an abstract process," I would say that T. S. Eliot has not glided through an abstract process in formulating the three discourses just cited—exposition consonant in vividness with his best use of metaphor—"the seabell's perpetual angelus" and the lines about standing at the "stern of the drumming liner, watching the furrow that widens behind us."

Of poetry, current at Oxford, W. H. Auden says in the *Letter to Lord Byron*, "Eliot spoke the still unspoken word,"

and in the tribute by him "To T. S. Eliot on His Sixtieth
Birthday," 1948, says:

> . . . it was you
> Who, not speechless from shock but finding the right
> Language for thirst and fear, did much to
> Prevent a panic.

The effect of Mr. Eliot's confidences, elucidations, and
precepts, I would say, is to disgust us with affectation; to
encourage respect for spiritual humility; and to encourage
us to do our ardent, undeviating best with the medium in
which we work.

The Cantos [1]

T H E S E Cantos are the epic of the farings of a literary mind.

The ghost of Homer sings. His words have the sound of the sea and the cadence of actual speech. *And So-shu churned in the sea, So-shu also.* [2] In Canto III we have an ideograph for the Far East, consisting of two parts:

> Green veins in the turquoise,
> Or, the gray steps lead up under the cedars.

The Cantos are concerned with *books, arms,* and *men of unusual genius.* They imply that there is nothing like the word-melody of the Greek; we have that of Latin also— Vergil and Ovid. One's ear can learn from the Latin something of quantity. " 'Not by the eagles only was Rome measured./Wherever the Roman speech was, there was Rome.'/Wherever the speech crept, there was mastery." The Cantos imply that there is pleasure to be had from Propertius and Catullus, that Catullus is very winning; it

---

[1] Review of Ezra Pound's A *Draft of XXX Cantos,* in *Poetry,* October 1931.
[2] Material quoted from the Cantos appears in italic or is set in small type; from other work, in double quotation marks.

is plain that in liking him, one has something of his attitude of mind. "Can we know Ovid," Mr. Pound asks in
his "Notes on Elizabethan Classicists," "until we find him
in Golding? . . . is not a new beauty created, an old beauty
doubled when the overchange is well done?" On returning
to Paris after seven years, *Knocking at empty rooms, seek-
ing for buried beauty,*" Mr. Pound is told by *A strange
concierge, in place of the gouty-footed,* that the friend he
asks about is dead. For the attar of friendship of one long
dead

> Dry casques of departed locusts
> speaking a shell of speech. . .

are not a substitute. Golding afforded "reality and par-
ticularization"; whereas Paris is a thing of *Words like the
locust-shells, moved by no inner being;* and Mr. Pound
thinks for a moment of the scarlet-curtain simile in the
"Flight from Hippomenes" in Ovid's *Metamorphoses,*
translated by Golding,[3] and murmurs, *The scarlet curtain
throws a less scarlet shadow.* This Paris Canto—VII—is one
of the best; the eleven last lines are memorable, stately.

It is apparent that the Latin line is quantitative. If poetics
allure, the Cantos will also show that in Provençal min-
strelsy we encounter a fascinating precision; the delicacy
and exactness of Arnaut Daniel, whose invention, the
sestina form, is "like a thin sheet of flame folding and in-
folding upon itself." In this tongue—you read it in manuscripts rather than in books—is to be found pattern. And
the Cantos show how the troubadours not only sang poems

[3] "As when a scarlet curtain streyned against a playstred wall
Doth cast like shadowe, making it seeme ruddye there-with all."

but *were* poems. Usually they were in love, with My Lady Battle if with no other, and were often successful, for in singing of love one sometimes finds it—especially when the *canzos* are good ones. And there were jealous husbands. Miguel de la Tour is most pleasing to Mr. Pound in what he says of Piere de Maensac, who carried off the wife of Bernart de Tierci. "The husband, in the manner of the golden Menelaus, demanded her much," and there was *Troy in Auvergnat*. But it happened often that the minstrel was thrown into prison or put himself there, like Bernart of Ventadorn, who sang of the lark and who "ended his days in the monastery of Dalon." In this connection, disparity in station, under which people suffer and are patient, is regrettable; Madonna Biancha Visconti was married by her uncle to a peasant; and the troubadours oftener than not were frustrated in love; they were poor and were usually more gifted than the men whose appurtenance they were. But things are sometimes reversed, as when a man of title falls in love with a tirewoman. And not always are people to be balked, as we see in the case of this Pedro the persistent, who came to reign, murdered the murderers of the tirewoman, and married the dug-up corpse. Pedro's ghost sings in Canto III and again in XXX.

Mr. Pound brings to his reading master-appreciation, and his gratitude takes two forms; he thanks the book and tells where you may see it. "Any man who would read Arnaut and the troubadours owes great thanks to Emil Lévy of Freiburg," he says in *Instigations*, "for his long work and his little dictionary (*Petit Dictionnaire Provençal-Français*, Karl Winter's Universitätsbuchhandlung, Heidelberg)." He sings of this in Canto XX—of the old man who at about

*6:30/ in the evening, . . . trailed half way across Freiburg/
before dinner, to see the two strips of copy.*

And as those who love books know, the place in which
one read a book or talked of it partakes of its virtue in recollection; so for Mr. Pound the cedars and new-mown hay and
far-off nightingale at Freiburg have the glamour of Provence.
He says (Canto XX):

> You would be happy for the smell of that place
> And never tired of being there, either alone
> Or accompanied.

And he intimates that no lover of books will do himself
the disservice of overlooking Lope de Vega, his "matchless
buoyancy, freshness," "atmosphere of earliest morning,"
"like that hour before the summer dawn, when the bracing
cool of the night still grips the air," his "sprightly spirit of
impertinence," his tenderness. In Canto III is echoed the
joke from the *Cid* about the gold—the two chests of sand
"covered with vermilion leather" and pawned with the pro-
viso that "they be not disturbed for a year"; and there are
echoes of the slumber song that speaks of angels a-flying.

As for Dante, even the mind most unsparing of itself will
not easily get all that is to be got from him. Books and arms.
Either is not necessarily a part of the other any more than
the books from the London Library that were taken to the
late war by T. E. Hulme and were buried by a shell in a dug-
out. But we enjoy Homer, Vergil, Dante, and what they had
to say about war. And arms are mentioned in the *Chanson
de Roland* and in Shakespeare. And we enjoy the Cantos in
which Mr. Pound sings of the wars between cities in an Italy
of unsanitary dungeons and great painting, and what he says

of diplomatic greed as disgusting and also comic; and in what he says of wigglings, split fees, tips, and self-interest; and of how

> Sigismundo, ally, come through an enemy force,
> To patch up some sort of treaty, passes one gate
> And they shut it before they open the next gate, and he says:
> "Now you have me,
>   Caught like a hen in a coop."

Speaking of Italy, we find in Canto XXVI a picture of Mr. Pound outside St. Mark's on one of his first visits to Venice, of which visit he says:

> And
> I came here in my youth
>   and lay there under the crocodile
> By the column . . .

To one looking up at it, it is small, like the silhouette of a lizard, this bronze crocodile, souvenir of Venetian acquisitiveness.

> And at night they sang in the gondolas
> And in the barche with lanthorns;
> The prows rose silver on silver
>   taking light in the darkness.

To return to fighting, "Dante fought at Campaldino, 'in the front rank,'" and "saw further military service," and other men of literary genius have survived war. Canto XVI alludes to Lord Byron, who once bore arms for Greece, though the canto alludes to him as wrapped in scarlet and resembling a funeral; not dead, merely drunk. But the drunkenness that is war! War such as this last:

> And Henri Gaudier went to it,
>   and they killed him.

Why cannot money and life go for beauty instead of for war and intellectual oppression? This question is asked more than once by the Cantos. Books and arms. Under the head of arms, as you will have noticed, come daggers—like Pedro's, and Giovanni Malatesta's sword that slew Paolo, the beautiful. Books, arms, men. To Dante antiquity was not a figment; nor is it to Mr. Pound, any more than Mme. Curie is a figment, or the man he knew in Manhattan,

> 24 E. 47th, when I met him,
> Doing job printing.

Men of unusual genius, *Both of ancient times and our own.* Of our own (Canto VII), Henry James

> Moves before me, phantom with weighted motion,
> *Grave incessu,* drinking the tone of things,
> And the old voice lifts itself
> > weaving an endless sentence.

And there was an exemplary American, favorable to music.

> "Could you," wrote Mr. Jefferson,
> "Find me a gardener
> Who can play the french horn?"

And the singer curses his country for being *Midas lacking a Pan!* To cite passages is to pull one quill from a porcupine. Mr. Pound took two thousand and more pages to say it in prose, and he sings it in a hundred-forty-two. The book is concerned with beauty. You must read it yourself; it has a power that is mind and is music; it comes with the impact of centuries and with the impact of yesterday. Amid the swarming madness of excellence, there is the chirping of "the young phoenix broods," the Chinese music, the slender bird-note that gives one no peace. "Great poets," Mr.

Pound says, "seldom make bricks without straw. They pile up all the excellences they can beg, borrow, or steal from their predecessors and contemporaries, and then set their own inimitable light atop the mountain." Of the Cantos, then, what is the master-quality? Scholastically, it is "concentrating the past on the present," as T. S. Eliot says; rhetorically, it is certitude; musically, it is range with an unerring ear. Note Cantos XIII, XVII, XXI, and XXX. And in all this "wealth of motive," this "*largesse*," this "intelligence," are there no flaws? Does every passage in this symphony "relieve, refresh, revive the mind of the reader— at reasonable intervals—with some form of ecstasy, by some splendour of thought, some presentation of sheer beauty, some lightning turn of phrase"? Not invariably. The "words affect modernity," says William Carlos Williams, "with too much violence (at times)—a straining after slang effects. . . . You cannot *easily* switch from Orteum to Peoria without violence (to the language). These images too greatly infest the Cantos."

Unprudery is overemphasized and secularity persists, refuted though this charge is by the prose praise of Dante: "His work is of that sort of art which is a key to the deeper understanding of nature and the beauty of the world and of the spirit"; "for the praise of that part of his worth which is fibre rather than surface, my mind is not yet ripe, nor is my pen skilled." Most of us have not the tongues of the spirit, but those who have, tell us that, by comparison, knowledge of the spirit of tongues is as insignificant as are the clothes worn by one in infancy. We share Mr. Pound's diffidence.

T. S. Eliot suspects Ezra Pound's philosophy of being antiquated. William Carlos Williams finds his "versifica-

tion *still* patterned after classic metres"; and, apropos of
"feminolatry," is not the view of woman expressed by the
Cantos older-fashioned than that of Siam and Abyssinia?
knowledge of the femaleness of *chaos,* of the *octopus,* of
Our mulberry leaf, woman, appertaining more to Turkey
than to a Roger Ascham? Nevertheless Mr. Pound likes
the denouement of *Aucassin and Nicolette,* and in comparing *Romeo and Juliet* with De Vega's *Castelvines y
Monteses,* sees "absolutely no necessity for the general
slaughter at the end of Shakespeare's play." He addresses the
lutanists in their own tongue (Canto VIII):

> "Ye spirits who of olde were in this land
> Each under Love, and shaken,
> Go with your lutes, awaken
> The summer within her mind,
> Who hath not Helen for peer,
> > Yseut nor Batsabe."

But, a practical man in these matters, he sees the need for
antidotes to "inebriation from the *Vita Nuova*"; namely,
Sir James Fraser and Rémy de Gourmont; one no longer
mistakes the singer's habiliment for his heart any more than
one acquainted with the prose of James Joyce would find
the bloom on the poems in *Chamber Music* artless.

What about Cantos XIV and XV? Let us hope that "Disgust with the sordid is but another expression of a sensitive-
ness to the finer thing."

Petty annoyances are magnified; when one is a beginner,
tribulation worketh impatience.

Stock oaths, and the result is ennui, as with the stock ad-
jective.

An annoyance by no means petty is the lack of an index.

And since the Cantos are scrupulous against half-truth and against *what had been thought for too long*—ought they not to suggest to those who have accepted Calvin by hearsay—or heresy—that one must make a distinction between Calvin the theologian and Calvin the man of letters? Or is Mr. Pound indifferent to wit from that quarter—as sailors in the Baltic are said not to shave when the wind is favorable?

Those who object to the Cantos' obscurity—who prefer the earlier poems—are like the victims of Calvin who have not read him. It may be true that the author's revisions make it harder, not easier, for hurried readers; but flame kindles to the eye that contemplates it. Besides, these *are* the earlier poems. A critic that would have us "establish axes of reference by knowing the *best of each kind of written thing*" has persisted to success; is saying something "in such a way that one cannot re-say it more effectively." Note the affinity with material commonly called sentimental, which in most writers becomes sickly and banal, and in the Cantos is kept keen and alive; and the tactility with which Mr. Pound enables us to relive antiquity: *Da Gama wore striped pants in Africa.* And he sets it "to paint" so that we may *see* what he says. The pale backgrounds are by Leonardo da Vinci; there are faces with the *eyes of Picasso*; the walls are by Mantegna. The yellow in Canto XVII, of the fawn and the broom, and the cerise grasshopper-wing, gain perhaps by contrast with a prevailing tendency, in the Cantos, to blue. *Malachite, green clear, and blue clear, blue-gray glass of the wave, Glare azure, Black snout of a porpoise.* The dramatist's eye that sees this, and *Cosimo's red leather note book* and the *big*

green account book and the lion whelps *vivos et piloses living and hairy, waves* . . . *holding their form/No light
reaching through them,*

> And the waters richer than glass,
> Bronze gold, the blaze over the silver,
> Dye-pots in the torch-light,

find the mechanistic world also "full of enchantments,"
"not only the light in the electric bulb, but the thought of
the current hidden in the air," "and the rose that his magnet
makes in the iron filings." And added to imagination is the
idiosyncratic force of the words—the terseness in which
some reflower and some are new. Of Mr. Pound and words,
Dr. Williams says, "He has taken them up—if it may be
risked—alertly, swiftly, but with feeling for the delicate
living quality in them, not disinfecting, scraping them, but
careful of the life." The skill that in the prose has been in-
comparably expert in epitomizing what others have bungled,
shows us that "you can be wholly precise in representing a
vagueness." This ambidextrous precision, born of integrity
and intrepidity, is the poet's revenge upon those "who refuse
to say what they think, if they do think," who are like those
who see nothing the matter with bad surgery. And allied
with veracity are translatorly qualities that nourish ingenuity in the possessor of them: a so unmixed zeal for essence
that no assaying of merits in rendering is a trouble; an independence that will not subscribe to superstition—to the
notion, for instance, that a text written in Greek is of necessity better than a text written in Latin. Even Homer can be
put characteristically into Latin. *Andreas Divus* "plucked

from a Paris stall" "gave him in Latin," *In officina Wecheli,*
1538,

> Caught up his cadence, word and syllable:
> "Down to the ships we went, set mast and sail,
>> Black keel and beasts for bloody sacrifice,
> Weeping we went."

And the English of Golding's Ovid is as good as the Latin.
"A master may be continually expanding his own tongue,
rendering it fit to bear some charge hitherto borne only by
some other alien tongue"; yet as Fontenelle said to Erasmus,
"If before being vain of a thing" men "should try to assure themselves that it really belonged to them, there would
be little vanity in the world."

The new in Mr. Pound, as in any author, hides itself from
the dull and is accentuated for the quick. Certain imple-
ments in use by James Joyce are approved: the pun, the
phonetic photography of dialect, propriety with vibrating
edge of impropriety, the wry jest—'Hélion t' 'Hélion. "All
artists who discover anything . . . must, in the course of
things, . . . push certain experiments beyond the right
curve of their art," Mr. Pound says, and some would say,
the facing in many directions as of a quadriga drawn by
centaurs, which we meet in the Cantos, puts strain on bi-
pedal understanding; there is love of risk; but the experienced
grafting of literature upon music is here very remarkable—
the resonance of color, allusions, and tongues sounding one
through the other as in symphonic instrumentation. Even if
one understood nothing, one would enjoy the musicianship.

Thus the book of the mandates:

Feb. 1422.

We desire that you our factors give to Zohanne of Rimini
our servant, six lire marchesini,

for the three prizes he has won racing our barbarisci,
at the rate we have agreed on. The races he has won
are the Modena, the San Petronio at Bologna
and the last race at San Zorzo.

> (Signed) Parisina Marchesa

Mr. Pound says, "Everyone has been annoyed by the difficulty of indicating the *exact* tone and rhythm with which
one's verse is to be read," but in the "capripedal" counterpoint of the above little fugue à la gigue he has put it beyond
our power to stumble. And there is discovery in the staccato
sound of the conclusion to Canto XXX, in the patterning
of the "y" in "thirty" on the "i" in *mori*:

> Il Papa mori.

> Explicit canto
> XXX

The master-quality throughout the Cantos is decision:

> SIGISMUNDUS HIC EGO SUM
> MALATESTA, FILIUS PANDULPHI, REX PRODITORUM

But however explicit the accents in the line, the fabric on
which the pattern is focused is indispensable to accuracy.
There is the effect sometimes, as in the medieval dance, of a
wheel spun one way and then the other; there is the sense
of a horse rushing toward one and turning, unexpectedly
rampant; one has stepped back but need not have moved.
Note the luster of a subtle slowing exactly calculated (Canto
V):

> Fades the light from the sea, and many things
> "Are set abroad and brought to mind of thee."

"The music of rhymes depends upon their arrangement,
not on their multiplicity." We are aware in the Cantos of

the skill of an ear with a faculty for rhyme in its most developed arrangements, but, like that of a Greek, against the vulgarity of rhyme; a mind aware of instruments—aware of "the circular bars of the Arabs, divided, like unjust mince pies, from centre to circumference," and of "the beautiful irregularities of the human voice." Whatever the training, however, "a man's rhythm" "will be, in the end, his own, uncounterfeiting, uncounterfeitable"; and in Canto XIII, in the symbolic discussion of the art of poetics, what is said is illustrated by the manner of saying:

> And Tseu-lou said, "I would put the defences in order,"
> And Khieu said, "If I were lord of a province
> I would put it in better order than this is."
> And Tchi said, "I would prefer a small mountain temple,
> With order in the observances,
>   with a suitable performance of the ritual,"
>
>   .   .   .
>
> And Kung said, "They have all answered correctly,
> That is to say, each in his nature."
>
>   .   .   .
>
> And Kung said, and wrote on the bo leaves:
>   "If a man have not order within him
> He can not spread order about him;
>
>   .   .   .
>
>   "Anyone can run to excesses,
> It is easy to shoot past the mark,
> It is hard to stand firm in the middle."

There is no easy way if you are to be a great artist; and the nature of one, in achieving his art, is different from the nature of another.

Mr. Pound, in the prose that he writes, has formulated his own commentary upon the Cantos. They are an armorial coat of attitudes to things that have happened in books and in life; they are not a shield but a coat worn by a man, as in the days when heraldry was beginning. He serves under Beauty, with the motto, Τό Καλόν. "Ordinary people," he says in his turtle poem, "touch me not." His art is his turtle-shell or snail house; it is all one animal moving together, and

> Who seeks him must be worse than blind,
> He and his house are so combined,
> If finding it he fails to find
> > its master.[4]

[4] "The Snail" by Cowper.

"Teach, Stir the Mind, Afford Enjoyment" [1]

OUR DEBT to Ezra Pound is prodigious for the effort he has made to share what he knows about writing and, in partic-ular, about rhythm and melody; most of all, for his insistence on liveness as opposed to deadness. "Make it new," he says. "Art is a joyous thing." He recalls "that sense of sudden growth we experience in the presence of the greatest works of art." The ode to *Hugh Selwyn Mauberley* applies of course to himself:

> For three years, out of key with his time,
> He strove to resuscitate the dead art

[1] From a series of commentaries on selected contemporary poets, Bryn Mawr, 1952.

Of poetry; to maintain "the sublime"
In the old sense. . . .

And, above all, it is the art of letters in America that he has wished to resuscitate. He says in "Cantico del Sole":

The thought of what America would be like
If the classics had a wide circulation
Troubles my sleep. . . .

America's imperviousness to culture irks him; but he is never as indignant as he is elated.

Instruction should be painless, he says, and his precept for writers is an epitome of himself: teach, stir the mind, afford enjoyment. (Cicero's *Ut doceat, ut moveat, ut delectet.*[2]) Hugh Kenner grants him his wish and says: "The Pound letters are weirdly written; they are nevertheless a treatise on creative writing, treasure-trove, *corpus aureum, mina de oro.* . . . The vivacity of these letters is enchanting." Mr. Kenner also says, "The whole key to Pound, the basis of his Cantos, his music, his economics and everything else, is the concern for exact definition"—a passion shared by T. S. Eliot, Mr. Kenner adds—"a quality which neither has defined." What is it? a neatening or cleancutness, to begin with, as caesura is cutting at the end (*caedo,* cut off). For Dante, it was making you see the thing that he sees, Mr. Pound says; and, speaking of Rimbaud, says there is "such

[2] See Kenneth Burke's "The Language of Poetry, 'Dramatistically' Considered," paper written for a symbolism seminar conducted in 1952–53 by the Institute for Religious and Social Studies, New York (*Chicago Review,* Fall 1954): "We would spin this discussion from Cicero's terms for the 'three offices of the orator.' (See *Orator, De Oratore,* and St. Augustine's use of this analysis of Christian persuasion in his *De Doctrina Christiana.*) First office: to teach or inform (*docere*). Second office: to please (*delectare*). Third office: to move or 'bend' (*movere, flectare*)."

firmness of coloring and such certitude." Pound admires
Chinese codifyings and for many a year has been ordering,
epitomizing, and urging explicitness, as when he listed "A
Few Don'ts" for Imagists:

> Direct treatment, economy of words; compose in the se-
> quence of the musical phrase rather than that of the metro-
> nome.
> The true poet is most easily distinguished from the false
> when he trusts himself to the simplest expression and writes
> without adjectives.
> No dead words or phrases.
> A thought should be expressed in verse at least as well as it
> could be expressed in prose. Great literature is language
> charged with meaning to the utmost possible degree. There
> is no easy way out.

Mr. Pound differentiates poetry as

> logopoeia (music of words),
> melopoeia (music of sound)—the music of rhymes,
>   he says, depends upon their arrangement, not
>   only on their multiplicity—and
> phanopoeia (casting images on the imagination).

Under the last head, one recalls the statement by Dante
that Beatrice walked above herself—*come una crana.* Confu-
cius says the fish moves on winglike foot; and Prior, in his
life of Edmund Burke, says Burke "had a peculiarity in his
gait that made him look as if he had two left legs." Affirming Coleridge's statement that "Our admiration of
a great poet is for a continuous undercurrent of feeling
everywhere present, but seldom anywhere a separate excitement," Mr. Pound says Dante "has gone living through Hell

and the words of his lament sob as branches beaten by the wind."

What is poetry? Dante said, "a song is a composition of words set to music." As for free verse, "it is *not* prose," Mr. Pound says. It is what we have "when the thing builds up a rhythm more beautiful than that of set metres"—as here:

> The birds flutter to rest in my tree,
>   and I think I have heard them saying,
> "It is not that there are no other men—,
> But we like this fellow the best. . . ."

In Dante, "we have blending and lengthening of the sounds, heavy beats, running and light beats," Mr. Pound says. "Don't make each line stop dead at the end. Let the beginning of the next line catch the rise of the rhythm wave, unless you want a longish definite pause." For example, the lines from "Envoi" in *Mauberley*, when he speaks of "her graces":

> I would bid them live
> As roses might, in magic amber laid,
> Red overwrought with orange and all made
> One substance and one colour
> Braving time.

This is the way in which to cement sound and thought. In *Mauberley*, also note the identical rhymes in close sequence without conspicuousness, of "Medallion":

> The face-oval beneath the glaze,
> Bright in its suave bounding-line, as,
> Beneath half-watt rays,
> The eyes turn topaz.

"Words," T. S. Eliot says, "are perhaps the hardest medium of all material of art. One must simultaneously express visual beauty, beauty of sound, and communicate a grammatical statement." We have in "her" a mundane word, but note the use made of it in Portrait, from "La Mère Inconnue" (*Exultations*):

> Nay! For I have seen the purplest shadows stand
> Always with reverent chere that looked on her,
> Silence himself is grown her worshipper
> And ever doth attend her in that land
> Wherein she reigneth, wherefore let there stir
> Naught but the softest voices, praising her.

Again, from Ezra Pound's translation of Guido Cavalcanti: "A Bernardo da Bologna,"

> And in that Court where Love himself fableth
> Telling of beauties he hath seen, he saith:
> This pagan and lovely woman hath in her
> All strange adornments that ever were.

William Carlos Williams is right. "Pound is not 'all poetry.' . . . But he has an ear that is unsurpassable." "Some poems," Mr. Pound himself says, "have form as a tree has form and some as water poured into a vase." He also says, quoting Arnold Dolmetsch and Mace: "Mark not the beat too much"—a precept essential to light rhyme and surprises within the line; but inapplicable to satire, as in W. S. Gilbert's *Pirates of Penzance*—the policemen:

> And yet when someone's near
> We manage to appear
> As unsusceptible to fear
> As anybody here.

"The churn, the loom, the spinning-wheel, the oars," Mr. Pound says, "are bases for distinctive rhythm which can never degenerate into the monotony of mere iambs and trochees"; and one notices in "Nel Biancheggiar" the accenting of "dies," in "but dies not quite":

> I feel the dusky softness whirr
> Of colour, as upon a dulcimer
>
>   .   .   .
>
> As when the living music swoons
> But dies not quite. . . . .

One notes in "Guido Invites You Thus" (*Exultations*) the placing of the pauses and quickened "flames of an altar fire":

> Lo, I have known thy heart and its desire;
> Life, all of it, my sea, and all men's streams
> Are fused in it as flames of an altar fire!

And "A Prologue" (*Canzoni*) has the same exactitude in variety:

> Shepherds and kings, with lambs and frankincense
> Go and atone for mankind's ignorance:
> Make ye soft savour from your ruddy myrrh.
> Lo, how God's son is turned God's almoner.

Unending emphasis is laid by Ezra Pound on honesty—on voicing one's own opinion. He is indignant that "trout should be submerged by eels." The function of literature, he says, is "to incite humanity to continue living; to ease the mind of strain; to feed it" (Canto XXV):

> What we thought had been thought for too long;
>
>   .   .   .
>
> We have gathered a sieve full of water.
>
>   .   .   .
>
> The dead words, keeping form.

We suffer from

> Noble forms lacking life,
>
> . . .
>
> The dead concepts, never the solid;

As for comprehension of what is set forth, the poet has a right to expect the reader, at least in a measure, to be able to complete poetic statement; and Ezra Pound never spoils his effects by over-exposition. He alludes as follows to the drowning of a Borgia:

> The bust outlasts the shrine;
> The coin, Tiberius.
>
> . . .
>
> John Borgia is bathed
> at last. And the cloak floated.

"As for *Cathay*, it must be pointed out," T. S. Eliot says, "that Pound is the inventor of Chinese poetry of our time"; and seeing a connection between the following incident and "the upper-middlebrow press," Hugh Kenner recalls that when Charles Münch offered Bach to the regiment, the commandant said, "Here, none of that mathematical music." One ventures, commits one's self, and if readers are not pleased, one can perhaps please one's self and earn that slender right to persevere.

"A poet's work," Mr. Eliot says, "may proceed along two lines of an imaginary graph; one of the lines being his conscious and continuous effort in technical excellence," and the other "his normal human course of development. Now and then the two lines may converge at a high peak, so that we get a masterpiece. That is to say, an accumulation of ex-

perience has crystallized to form material of art, and years
of work in technique have prepared an adequate medium;
and something results in which medium and material, form
and content, are indistinguishable."

In *The Great Digest and Unwobbling Pivot* of Confu-
cius, as in his *Analects*, Ezra Pound has had a theme of
major import. *The Great Digest* makes emphatic this lesson: He who can rule himself can govern others; he who
can govern others can rule the kingdom and families of the
Empire.

> The men of old disciplined themselves.
> Having attained self-discipline they set their houses in order.
> Having order in their own homes, they brought good govern-
> ment to their own state.
> When their states were well governed, the empire was brought
> into equilibrium.

We have in the *Digest*, content that is energetic, novel, and
deep: "If there be a knife of resentment in the heart or
enduring rancor, the mind will not attain precision; under
suspicion and fear it will not form sound judgment, nor will
it, dazzled by love's delight nor in sorrow and anxiety, come
to precision." As for money, "Ill got, ill go." When others
have ability, if a man "shoves them aside, he can be called
a real pest." "The archer when he misses the bullseye, turns
and seeks the cause of error in himself." There must be no
rationalizing. "Abandon every clandestine egoism to realize
the true root." Of the golden rule, there are many variants
in the *Analects*: "Tze-kung asked if there was a single principle that you could practise through life to the end. He
said sympathy; what you don't want, don't inflict on an-

other" (Book Fifteen, xxiii). "Require the solid of yourself, the trifle of others" (Book Fifteen, xiv). "The proper man brings men's excellence to focus, not their evil qualities" (Book Twelve, xvi). "I am not worried that others do not know me; I am worried by my incapacity" (Book Fourteen, xxxii). Tze-chang asked Kung-tze about maturity. Kung-tze said: To be able to practise five things would humanize the whole empire—sobriety (*serenitas*), magnanimity, sticking by one's word, promptitude (in attention to detail), kindliness (*caritas*). As for "the problem of style. Effect your meaning. Then stop" (Book Fifteen, xl).

In "Salvationists," Mr. Pound says:

> Come, my songs, let us speak of perfection—
> We shall get ourselves rather disliked.

We shall get ourselves disliked and very much liked, because the zest for perfection communicates its excitement to others.

W . H . AUDEN [1]

WE SURELY have in W. H. Auden—in his prose and verse—stature in diversity. It is instructive, moreover, to see in him the abilities he admires in others—the "capacity for drawing general conclusions," mentioned by him as "the extraordinary, perhaps unique merit" of de Tocqueville; and together with clinical attention to cause and effect, a gift for the conspectus. After speaking of de Tocqueville as a counterrevolutionary—i.e., one who has no wish to return to the condition which preceded revolution—he says, "The body knows nothing of freedom, only of necessities; these are the same for all bodies," and "insofar as we are bodies, we are revolutionaries; insofar, however, as we are also souls and minds, we are or ought to be *counter*revolutionaries." He feels that "The books of de Tocqueville belong together with Thucydides, the Seventh Epistle of Plato, and the plays of Shakespeare, in the small group of the indispensable."

Mr. Auden embodies in his work many gratitudes. His *New Year Letter*, addressed to Elizabeth Mayer—"This *aide-mémoire* . . ./This private minute to a friend"—constitutes a veritable reading list of those to whom he feels a debt, and —an even better compliment—he has adopted various of their idiosyncrasies, as in the dedication to *Another Time* he recalls Blake's

<hr/>

[1] From a series of commentaries on selected contemporary poets, Bryn Mawr, 1952.

84

Till I Will be overthrown
Every eye must weep alone.

In the *New Year Letter*, he says that Blake

. . . even as a child would pet
The tigers Voltaire never met,

he feels that he has a debt to young Rimbaud,

Skilful, intolerant and quick,
Who strangled an old rhetoric,

and he says,

There DRYDEN sits with modest smile,
The master of the middle style.

If by the middle style he means the circumspectly auda-
cious, he too is possessed of it.

He directs a warm glance toward Catullus,

Conscious CATULLUS who made all
His gutter-language musical.

Nor is Mr. Auden himself too fettered to use "who," "he,"
"the," or "which" as an end rhyme. He sees Voltaire facing
him "like a sentinel." He says, "Yes, the fight against the
false and the unfair was always worth it." He feels a debt to

HARDY whose Dorset gave much joy
To one unsocial English boy,

and Shakespeare? One is

. . . warned by a great sonneteer
Not to sell cheap what is most dear.

"Only by those who reverence it, can life be mastered."
There is a suggestion of *Murder in the Cathedral* about that;

as about the following reflection from A *Christmas Oratorio*, "The Temptation of St. Joseph":

> Sin fractures the Vision, not the Fact; for
> The Exceptional is always usual
> And the Usual exceptional.
> To choose what is difficult all one's days
> As if it were easy, that is faith. Joseph, praise.

Mr. Auden has a fondness for the seven-syllable-line rhythm,

> Now the ragged vagrants creep
> Into crooked holes to sleep;

the rhythm of

> Where the bee sucks, there suck I:
> In a cowslip's bell I lie . . .

and "Shame the eager with ironic praise" recalls Pope.

We infer approval of Ogden Nash in "a stranded fish to be kind to" and "had he a mind to"; again, in "Are You There?":

> Each lover has some theory of his own
> About the difference between the ache
> Of being with his love and being alone.

Appreciative of others he can afford to be. He could never sound as much like others as others sound like him. His collected poems, moreover, constitute, as Louise Bogan says, "the most minute dissection of the spiritual illness of our day that any modern poet, not excluding T. S. Eliot, has given us." He is a notable instance of the poet whose scientific predilections do not make him less than a poet—

who says to himself, I must know. In "The Walking Tour,"
he speaks of how

> The future shall fulfil a surer vow
>
> .   .   .
>
> Not swooping at the surface still like gulls
> But with prolonged drowning shall develop gills.

Commenting on Maria Edgeworth's Letters, Cecilia
Townsend says, "Without sorrow, the spirit dwindles." [2]
"Why are people neurotic?" Mr. Auden asks. "Because they
refuse to accept suffering." And in one of his *Cornelia Street
Dialogues* with Howard Griffin, he says, "suffering plays a
greater part than knowledge" in our acts of the will. One
can say, "I *should do* this. Will I do it? A part of the mind
looks on; a part decides. Also one must not discount Grace."
Mr. Griffin says: "You mean supernatural intervention—
the light that appeared to Saul on the road to Damascus?"
Mr. Auden: "Not really supernatural. . . . It may be perfectly natural. It depends on intensification of normal
powers of sensitivity and contemplation."

In an address to the Grolier Club (October 24, 1946),
Mr. Auden said, "Without an exception, the characters in
Henry James are concerned with moral choices. *The Beast
in the Jungle* is . . . the shrinking of the subject's sovereign
will from decisive choice. . . . The interest itself is in the
freedom of the will. Deny this freedom . . . and your interest vanishes." We have a debt to Mr. Auden for this
emphasis put on "denial of free will and moral responsibility" as "a recent feature of our novels." Why must we "see

---

[2] *The Spectator*, October 3, 1931.

ourselves," he asks, "as a society of helpless victims, shady
characters and displaced persons, . . . as heroes without
honor or history—heroes who succumb so monotonously to
temptation that they cannot truly be said to be tempted at
all?" The thought of choice as compulsory is central to
everything that he writes. "Of what happens when men
refuse to accept the necessity of choosing and are terrified
of or careless about their freedom, we now have only too
clear a proof," he said in 1941. "The will, decision, and the
consequences—there is no separating them." His "Star of
the Nativity" (A *Christmas Oratorio*) says:

> Descend into the fosse of Tribulation,
> Take the cold hand of Terror for a guide;
>
> .   .   .
>
> But, as the huge deformed head rears to kill,
> Answer its craving with a clear I Will;

"In War Time" makes emphatic

> The right to fail that is worth dying for.

Home is

> A sort of honour, not a building site,
> Wherever we are, when, if we choose, we might
> Be somewhere else, yet trust that we have chosen right.

And we have in the Notes to Part III of the *New Year
Letter*:

> I'm only lost until I see
> I'm lost because I want to be.

We must make "free confession of our sins." Humility,
alas, can border on humiliation. In the *New Year Letter*,
alluding to great predecessors, he asks, "Who . . .

Is not perpetually afraid
That he's unworthy of his trade,

. . .

Who ever rose to read aloud
Before that quiet attentive crowd
And did not falter as he read,
Stammer, sit down, and hang his head?

"Cognition," he says, "is always a specific historic act, accompanied by hope and fear."

How hard it is to set aside
Terror, concupiscence and pride.

Sin, fear, lust, pride. "The basis of pride," Mr. Auden says
in "Dialogue I," is to be found in "lack of security, anxiety,
and defiance; . . . says pride can be defined as a form of despair." And in the *New Year Letter* he says to the Devil:

You have no positive existence,
Are only a recurrent state
Of fear and faithlessness and hate,
That takes on from becoming me
A legal personality,

. . .

We hoped; we waited for the day
The State would wither clean away,

. . .

Meanwhile at least the layman knows
That none are lost so soon as those

. . .

Afraid to be themselves, or ask
What acts are proper to their task,

And that a tiny trace of fear
Is lethal in man's atmosphere.

Aware that Aladdin has the magic lamp that "Can be a sesame to light," he says:

Poor cheated Mephistopheles,
Who think you're doing as you please
In telling us by doing ill
To prove that we possess free will.

We have this metaphor of missed logic again in *The Rake's Progress*, where Nick Shadow leads Tom astray by suggesting that he is freed by disregarding passion and reason and marrying a freak. Choice is open to us each, and in *The Sea and the Mirror*, Alonso says:

Learn from your dreams what you lack,

. . .

Believe your pain: praise the scorching rocks
For their desiccation of your lust,
Thank the bitter treatment of the tide
For its dissolution of your pride,
That the whirlwind may arrange your will
And the deluge release it to find
The spring in the desert, the fruitful
Island in the sea, where flesh and mind
Are delivered from mistrust.

Similarly, Sebastian says:

O blessed be bleak Exposure on whose sword,
Caught unawares, we prick ourselves alive!

. . .

The sword we suffer is the guarded crown.

In his preface to *The Sea and the Mirror*, Mr. Auden quotes
Emily Brontë:

> And am I wrong to worship where
> Faith cannot doubt nor Hope despair
> Since my own soul can grant my prayer?
> Speak, God of Visions, plead for me
> And tell why I have chosen thee.

"Happiness does not depend," he says, "on power but on
love." "The person must begin by learning to be objective
about his Subjectivity"; so that "love is able to take the
place of hate." And in A *Christmas Oratorio:*

> The choice to love is open till we die.

. . .

> O Living Love replacing phantasy.

The patriot may then ("Epithalamion," *Collected Shorter
Poems*)

> Feel in each conative act
> Such a joy as Dante felt
> When, a total failure in
> An inferior city, he,
> Dreaming out his anger, saw
> All the scattered leaves of fact
> Bound by love.

"The Meditation of Simeon" (A *Christmas Oratorio*)
would have us see "the tragic conflict of Virtue with Necessity" as "no longer confined to the Exceptional Hero. Every
invalid is Roland defending the narrow pass against hope-
less odds; every stenographer is Brunhilde refusing to renounce her lover's ring which came into existence" through
the power of renunciation; and, redefining the hero, Mr.

Auden's introduction to the Brothers Grimm says: "The third son who marries the princess and inherits the kingdom is not a superman with exceptional natural gifts." He "succeeds not through his own merit, but through the assistance of Divine Grace. His contribution is, first, a humility which admits that he cannot succeed without Grace; secondly, a faith which believes that Grace will help him, so that when the old beggar asks for his last penny, that is, when humanly speaking he is dooming himself to fail, he can give it away; and lastly, a willingness . . . to accept suffering. . . . From tale after tale we learn, not that wishing is a substitute for action, but that wishes for good and evil are terribly real and not to be indulged in with impunity." But, in the "Journey to Iceland," Mr. Auden asks:

> "Where is the homage? when
> Shall justice be done? O who is against me?
> Why am I always alone?"

"Aloneness is man's real condition," he says; and as for justice, "The artist does not want to be accepted by others, he wants to accept his experience of life, which he cannot do until he has translated his welter of impressions into an order; the public approval he desires is not for himself but for his works, to reassure him that the sense he believes he has made of experience is indeed sense and not a self-delusion." [3]

"Lonely we were though never left alone," he says. We see loneliness "sniffing the herb of childhood" and finding

---

[3] *Partisan Review*, April 1950, reviewing *The Paradox of Oscar Wilde* by George Woodcock. To Oscar Wilde, Mr. Auden says, "Writing was a bore because it was only a means of becoming known and invited out, a preliminary to the serious job of spell-binding."

home a place "where shops have names" and "crops grow ripe"; and "In Praise of Limestone" (*Nones*) he reminds himself of

> . . . rounded slopes
> With their surface fragrance of thyme and beneath
> A secret system of caves and conduits; . . .

indeed says,

> . . . when I try to imagine a faultless love
> Or the life to come, what I hear is the murmur
> Of underground streams, what I see is a limestone landscape.

In the essay on Henry James—already referred to—he also says, "It is sometimes necessary for sons to leave the family hearth; it may well be necessary at least for intellectuals to leave their country as it is for children to leave their homes, not to get away from them, but to re-create them"; adding, however, that "those who become expatriate out of hatred for their homeland are as bound to the past as those who hate their parents." Having, like James, left the family hearth, an exile—"to keep the silences at bay" —must "cage/His pacing manias in a worldly smile" ("Vocation," *The Double Man*). It is not, however, a case of wishing nothing to be hard.

"A problem which is too easy," Mr. Auden says, "is as unattractive as a problem which is senseless or impossible. In playing a game, the excitement lies not in winning but in just-winning, and just-losing is almost as good as winning, and the same surely is true for thinking." Alluding to superficial or hasty persons, he says in "Our Bias":

> How wrong they are in being always right.
>   . . .

> For they, it seems, care only for success:
> While we choose words according to their sound
> And judge a problem by its awkwardness.

"A favorite game of my youth," he says, "was building dams; the whole afternoon was spent in building up what in the end was destroyed in a few seconds."

As offsetting the tribulations of life and a sense of injustice, one recalls Wallace Stevens' emphasis on the imagination as delivering us from our "bassesse." This, poetry should do; and W. H. Auden quotes Professor R. G. Collingwood as saying, "Art is not magic, but a mirror in which others may become conscious of what their own feelings really are. It mirrors defects and it mirrors escape"—affirmed in "The Composer" (*Collected Shorter Poems*):

> You alone, alone, O imaginary song,
> Are able to say an existence is wrong
> And pour out your forgiveness like a wine.

Thinking of W. H. Auden the person, one recalls the *Letter to Lord Byron:*

> But indecision broke off with a clean-cut end
> One afternoon in March at half-past three
> When walking in a ploughed field with a friend;
> Kicking a little stone, he turned to me
> And said, 'Tell me, do you write poetry?'
> I never had, and said so, but I knew
> That very moment what I wished to do.

"He dramatizes everything he touches," Louise Bogan says—as in "Under Which Lyre" (*Nones*),

> Our intellectual marines,
> Landing in little magazines
> Capture a trend

He sees "The bug whose view is baulked by grass," and our discarded acts

> Like torn gloves, rusted kettles,
> Abandoned branchlines, worn lop-sided
> Grindstones buried in nettles.

The recitative to *Night Mail*—the British documentary film on the nonstop express from London to Edinburgh—is drama without a break:

> As it rushes by the farmhouse no one wakes
> But a jug in a bedroom gently shakes.

Poets are musicians, and Mr. Auden's "In Praise of Limestone" says that one's "greatest comfort is music," "Which can be made anywhere and is invisible"; unlike

> The beasts who repeat themselves, or a thing like water
> Or stone whose conduct can be predicted . . .

A poet is susceptible to "elegance, art, fascination," and words demonstrate the appetite for them which made them possible:

> Altogether elsewhere, vast
> Herds of reindeer move across
> Miles and miles of golden moss,
> Silently and very fast.

That Mr. Auden is a virtuoso of rhythms we see in Ariel's refrain, "I," to Caliban ("Postscript," *The Sea and the Mirror*)—rivaling in attraction Herbert's "Heaven's Echo":

> Weep no more but pity me,
> Fleet persistent shadow cast
> By your lameness, caught at last,
> Helplessly in love with you,

Elegance, art, fascination,
  Fascinated by
  Drab mortality;
Spare me a humiliation
  To your faults be true:
I can sing as you reply
        . . . I [Echo by the Prompter]

And the next verse ends:

I will sing if you will cry
        . . . I

And the last verse:

What we shall become,
One evaporating sigh.
        . . . I

Urgency of a different sort we have in "Many Happy Returns (For John Rettger)":

I'm not such an idiot
As to claim the power
To peer into the vistas
  Of your future, still
I'm prepared to guess you
Have not found your life as
Easy as your sister's
  And you never will.

"One Circumlocution" (*Nones*) masters the art of rapt celerity:

Speak well of moonlight on a winding stair,
Of light-boned children under great green oaks;
The wonder, yes, but death should not be there.

Could the skill of the pauses be better, in "To You Simply"?

> Fate is not late,
> Nor the speech rewritten,
> Nor one word forgotten,
> Said at the start
> About heart,
> By heart, for heart.

And, superlatively accomplished, there is Poem XI in *Songs and Other Musical Pieces*:

> Lay your sleeping head, my love,
> Human on my faithless arm;
> Time and fevers burn away
> Individual beauty from
> Thoughtful children, and the grave
> Proves the child ephemeral:

The emphasis on "from" corroborates an impression that Mr. Auden is exceptional, if not alone, in imparting propriety to words separated from the words to which they belong. He has notably, moreover, a faculty for keeping a refrain from falling flat, as where in *A Christmas Oratorio* the Wise Men say, "Love is more serious than Philosophy"; reinforcing interior rhymes, we have intermittently the variant on "y" as a refrain—apathy, deny; tyranny, occupy; certainty, anarchy, spontaneity, enemy, energy, die; phantasy, by, and "Time is our choice of How to love and Why" —a device of great dignity.

As preface to his *Collected Poetry*, Mr. Auden says: "In the eyes of every author, I fancy, his own past work falls into four classes. First, the pure rubbish which he regrets ever having conceived; second—for him the most painful—the good ideas which his incompetence or impatience prevented from coming to much ("The Orators" seems to me such a case of the fair notion fatally injured); third, the pieces he has nothing against except their lack of importance; these must inevitably form the bulk of any collection since, were he to limit it to the fourth class alone, to those poems for which he is honestly grateful, his volume would be too depressingly slim."

Destined for the last category, surely, is *The Double Man*—particularly its *New Year Letter*, written in octosyllabic couplets with an occasional triplet, a diagnosis of the spiritual illness of our day and a landmark in literature. Here, as in the *Letter to Lord Byron*, Mr. Auden has chosen a form "large enough to swim in," and in it discusses our quest for freedom; we being—as epitomized by Montaigne on the title page—"double in ourselves, so that what we believe we disbelieve, and cannot rid ourselves of what we condemn." The Double Man asks (*New Year Letter* and Notes):

> Who built the Prison State?
> Free-men hiding from their fate.
> Will wars never cease?
> Not while they leave themselves in peace.

Therefore:

> The situation of our time
> Surrounds us like a baffling crime.
>
>   . . .
>
> Yet where the force has been cut down
> To one inspector dressed in brown,
> He makes the murderer whom he pleases
> And all investigation ceases.

"Peace will never be won," Mr. Dulles insists, "if men reserve for war their greatest effort"; as "we wage the war we are," Mr. Auden says; and not having waged it well, find ourselves waging the other kind also; from Spain to Siberia, from Ethiopia to Iceland; irresponsibleness having brought about

> The Asiatic cry of pain,
>
> . . .
>
> The Jew wrecked in the German cell,
> Flat Poland frozen into hell.

We are in a "coma of waiting, just breathing," because of our acedia or moral torpor,

> And all that we can always say
> Is: true democracy begins
> With free confession of our sins.

"Dante . . . showed us what evil is; not . . . deeds that must be punished, but our lack of faith." For "volunteers," it is "the penitential way that forces our wills to be freed," hell's fire being "the pain to which we go if we refuse to suffer."

When liberty has been recognized as "a gift with which to serve, enlighten, and enrich," then man is not in danger of being "captured by his liberty"; girls are not "married off to typewriters," children are not "inherited by slums"; and instead of terror, pride, and hate, we have faith, humility, and love. Just now, however, "with swimming heads and hands that shake," we watch the devil trying to destroy the root of freedom—that "absence of all dualities" that grows from "the roots of all togetherness," for "no man by himself has life's solution." "The Prince that Lies," he who

> . . . controls
> The moral assymetric souls

> The either-ors, the mongrel halves
> Who find truth in a mirror, laughs.

He "knows the bored will not unmask him." Mr. Auden is
not bored and has here met the devil with a deadly and
magnificent clarity. "The great schismatic . . . hidden in
his hocus-pocus" has "the gift of double focus," but

> . . . torn between conflicting needs,
> He's doomed to fail if he succeeds,

> . . .

> If love has been annihilated
> There's only hate left to be hated.

Understating his art as "The fencing wit of an informal
style," Mr. Auden has taken a leaf from Pope and devised
the needful complement whereby things forgot are hence-
forth known; and with the apparently effortless continuity
of the whale or porpoise in motion, he evolves constantly
entertaining treatment, resorting to varied terminology—
Greek, Latin, English, or other—presenting what he has to
say, with that crowning attraction, as he uses it, paradox at
its compactest.

An enemy to primness, Mr. Auden sometimes requires
that we enjoy "the Janus of a joke" at our expense, as when
he relegates the feminine to Laocoön status:

> Das weibliche that bids us come
> To find what we're escaping from.

And he is laughing at us also when he rhymes "ideas" with
"careers," "delta" with "skelter," and "Madonnas" with
"honors."

It is sad that we should be "the living dead" beneath
selfishness and ingratitude; that "few have seen Jesus," and
so many "Judas the Abyss." Persuading us to "show an
affirming flame" rather than "the negative way through
Time," and to believe that the cure for either tribulation or
temptation is humility, these New Year thoughts

> Convict our pride of its offence
> In all things, even penitence.

For we have here, despite much about the devil, a poem of
love and things of heaven—with a momentum of which
Buxtehude or Bach need not be ashamed, the melodic en-
tirety being something at which to marvel.

Inconvenienced, aided, attacked, or at large; a wave-worn
Ulysses, a Jerome among his documents; a misinterpreted
librettist; or a publisher's emissary insistently offered at
luncheon a dish of efts, Mr. Auden continues resolute. He
has a mission. Kimon Friar says, "There is an impersonality,
it seems to me . . . at the very center of Auden's style and
thinking, a veritable Ark of the Lord in which may be
housed the Holy Spirit or—to the unbaptized eye—state
the matter in accordance with your nature." [4] Education
and tribulation certainly have not been wasted on Mr.
Auden. His leaf does not wither; his technical proficiencies
deepen. In "The Shield of Achilles," he says he saw

> a ragged urchin, aimless and alone,—who'd never heard
> of any world where promises are kept,
> or one could weep because another wept.

[4] *Poetry*, May 1944.

Even a tinge of "greed" makes him "very ill indeed." His studies of Henry James and of Poe show to what heights of liberality he can rise. As a champion of justice, he will always have a champion in the pages he has penned; and as the Orpheus of our mountains, lakes, and plains, will always have his animals.

THE DIAL: A RETROSPECT[1]

AS GROWTH-RINGS in the cross section of a tree present a differentiated record of experience, successive editorial modifications of a magazine adjoin rather than merge; but the later *Dial* shared, or thought it shared, certain objectives of its predecessors.[2] It is that *Dial* which I know best, and when asked about it recollections spring up, of manuscripts, letters, people.

I think of the compacted pleasantness of those days at 152 West Thirteenth Street; of the three-story brick building with carpeted stairs, fireplace and white-mantelpiece rooms, business office in the first story front parlor, and in gold-leaf block letters, THE DIAL, on the windows to the right of the brownstone steps leading to the front door.

[1] *Partisan Review*, January-February, 1942.

[2] *The Dial*, founded in 1840 with Margaret Fuller as editor, Emerson as next editor, and Oliver Wendell Holmes, Hawthorne, and others as contributors, was discontinued after four years. In 1880 it was re-established by Francis F. Browne of Chicago, but in 1917 there was a change in editorial policy. The publication offices were moved to New York, and as a fortnightly with socially humanitarian emphasis, it was varyingly edited, first by George Bernard Donlin, then by Robert Morss Lovett, with Thorstein Veblen, Helen Marot, Randolph Bourne, Van Wyck Brooks, Harold Stearns, and others as contributing editors. In 1920 it was refashioned and brought out as a non-political monthly by Scofield Thayer, editor, and J. S. Watson, president, with Lincoln MacVeagh as treasurer—and was entitled *The Dial*, The Dial Publishing Company Inc. being the full title of the company, as it had been of the fortnightly *Dial*. The Dial Press, it might be noted, was not synonymous with it but a separate organization. Then, after having Stewart Mitchell as managing editor, followed by—though not always with the same title—Gilbert Seldes, Alyse Gregory, Kenneth Burke, and Marianne Moore, it was discontinued with the July issue, 1929.

There was the flower-crier in summer, with his slowly moving wagon of pansies, petunias, ageratum; of a man with straw-*ber*-ies for sale; or a certain fishman with pushcart-scales, and staccato refrain so unvaryingly imperative, summer or winter, that Kenneth Burke's parenthetic remark comes back to me—"I think if he stopped to sell a fish my heart would skip a beat."

I recall a visiting editor's incredulity when I said, "To me it's a revel," after being asked if I did not find reading manuscript tiresome—manuscripts meaning the requested, the volunteered, and the recommended; that third and sometimes uneasy entrant inducing a wish, not infrequently, that the roles of sponsor and author might be interchanged, as when in a letter of introduction a (Persian, I think) typographic neighbor wrote us, "In the country where I came from, the people say: 'Ham Liyarat, ham Tújarat'—Both pilgrimage and business, and so it is. Miss Z would like to have you see some of her poems."

Before being associated with *The Dial* editorially, I had been a subscriber, and still feel the impact of such writing as the W. B. Yeats reminiscences—"Four Years," "More Memories," and "An Autobiographic Fragment"; Paul Valéry's "An Evening with M Teste"; Mary Butts' "Speed the Plow"; D. H. Lawrence's sketches, "Rex" and "Adolph." I recall the aplomb of "Thus to Revisit," by Ford Madox Ford and the instructively mannerless manner of W. C. Blum's pages on Rimbaud; the photograph of Rimbaud as a child, reproduced next the translation of *A Season in Hell*; and Julien Benda's statement in *Belphegor*, "The problem of art is to discipline emotion without losing it." There was the continually surprising work of E. E. Cummings; William Carlos Williams' insurrectious brio; the exciting unconformity of the "Bantams in Pine-Woods" poems by Wallace Stevens. Thomas Mann's "German Letter" was for us a commentary on his fiction, as Ezra Pound's "Paris Letter" and T. S. Eliot's "London Letter" italicized their poetry. I recall the strong look of H. D.'s "Helios" on the page, and my grateful skepticism in receiving her suggestion that I offer work also.

Among the pictures, as intensives on the text, were three verdure-tapestry-like woodcuts by Galanis; Rousseau's lion among lotuses; "The Philosophers" by Stuart Davis; Adolph Dehn's "Viennese Coffee House"; and Kuniyoshi's curious "Heifer"—the forehead with a star on it of separate whorled strokes like propeller fins; Ernest Fiene, Charles Sheeler, Arthur Dove, John Marin, Georgia O'Keefe, Max Weber, Carl Sprinchorn, the Zorachs, and Bertram Hartman; Wyndham Lewis, Brancusi, Lachaise, Elie Nadelman, Picasso and Chirico, Cocteau line drawings, and Seurat's "Circus."

Such titles as "Sense and Insensibility," "Engineering with Words," "The American Shyness"; and the advertising —especially some lines "Against the Faux Bon" and "technique" in lieu of "genius"—seemed to say, "We like to do this and can do it better than anyone else could"; and I was self-warned to remain remote from so much rightness; finding also in Alyse Gregory's delicately lethal honesty something apart from the stodgy world of mere routine.

There was for us of the staff, whatever the impression outside, a constant atmosphere of excited triumph; and from editor or publisher, inherent fireworks of parenthetic wit too good to print.

In analyzing D. H. Lawrence's social logic, one usually disagrees with him, but I remember the start of pleasure with which I came on his evocation of violets, in the introduction to his *Pansies*: "Pensées, like pansies, have their roots in the earth, and in the perfume there stirs still the faint grim scent of under-earth. Certainly in pansy-scent and in violet-scent it is so; the blue of the morning mingled with the corrosive smoulder of the ground." Typical of W. B. Yeats' wisely unaccommodating intensity was his article on "The Death of Synge": "Synge was the rushing up of buried fire, an explosion of all that had been denied or refused, a furious impartiality, indifferent turbulent sorrow. Like Burns' his work was to say all that people did not want to have said."

And there were our at times elusive foreign correspondents: commenting from Germany, Thomas Mann; from Italy, Raffaello Piccoli; from Madrid, Ortega y Gasset; from Vienna, Hugo von Hofmannsthal; from Dublin, John Eglinton; from London, Raymond Mortimer;[3] from Paris, Paul Morand;[4] from Russia, Maxim Gorki—the foregoing, "active." And Bela Belazs (Hungary) and Otaker Fisher (Prague)—"inactive." Those were days when, as Robert Herring has said, things were opening out, not closing in.

I recall the explicit manual of duties with which the office was provided; and despite occasional editorial remonstrance, the inviolateness—to us—of our "contributing editor-critics," Gilbert Seldes (The Theatre); Henry Mc-Bride (Modern Art); Paul Rosenfeld and later Kenneth Burke (Music). Even recklessly against the false good, they

[3] Succeeding T. S. Eliot.
[4] Succeeding Ezra Pound.

surely did represent *The Dial* in "encouraging a tolerance for fresh experiments and opening the way for a fresh understanding of them."

Rivaling manuscript in significance were the letters; indivisible as art in some instances from their authors' published work. The effect of vacuum silence and naturalness in a note or two from D. H. Lawrence belongs for me with Mabel Dodge Luhan's statement, " 'Inessentials' seemed deadly to him who knew how to savor a piece of crusty bread on the side of a hill."

11 Feb 1929

> % Signor G. Orioli
> 6 Lungarno Corsini
> Florence Italy

Dear Marianne Moore

. . . I should have liked to see you in New York—but how was I to know you would like to see me!—many people don't. . . . We are staying here in Bandol near Marseille a little longer, then going back to Italy—so will you write me there, if you get the poems. And many greetings.—

Regarding my statement about the Pensées: there are lines in the book, that are the outcome of certain hurts and I am not saying that in every case the lines themselves leave no shadow of hurt. . . .

18 April 1929

Dear Marianne Moore

. . . I like the little group you chose—some of my favorites. . . . I think I shall withdraw that introduction from the book form—so you just keep any part of it you wish, & use it with your group of poems, as you wish. . . .

I knew some of the poems would offend you. But then some part of life must offend you too, and even beauty has its thorns and its nettle-stings and its poppy-poison. Noth-

ing is without offense, & nothing should be: if it is part of
life, & not merely abstraction.

We must stay in this island a while, but my address is
best c/ G. Orioli.

All good wishes
D. H. Lawrence

And from Paul Valéry in reply to a letter about his
*Introduction to the Method of Leonardo da Vinci: Note
and Digression, Part I: ". . .* I am very pleased to hear you
have found some spiritual refreshment in a work which so
many readers feel a little too much hard and bitter tasted
for common sense. But lucidity and will of lucidity lead
their passionate lover in crystal abysses deeper than old
Erebus. . . ."

Besides humor in our correspondence, there was satire,
as in A. E.'s reply to a suggestion that it was a long time
since he had sent us work, "Hawks should not prey upon
hawks." And an ostensible formality of our own, concocted
by Kenneth Burke, recurs to me—the answer to an advertising manager who complained that if books which had
received long reviews and unanimous approbation else-
where were to be damned at *The Dial* by brief notices and
faint praise, might they not be damned somewhat more
promptly? To this complaint from an acquaintance of Mr.
Burke's who had not foreseen that someone he knew might
be answering it, Mr. Burke said, "Why not give *The Dial*
credit? As you have said, under our silence the book went
through five editions. Now that we have spoken there may
never be a sixth. Further, we are happy to learn that
whereas we had feared that our 'Briefer Mention' was a
week or two late, the continued success of the book has

kept our comment green. We are, you might say, reviewing
a reprint—a courtesy not all gazettes will afford you. . . .
And are you, after all, so sure that a book benefits by having the reviews all let off at once like something gone
wrong in the arsenal, followed by an eternity of charred
silence!"

And we were not without academic loyalty in the guise
of reproof, one complainant who had been writing some
very good verse taking us to task about a review which he
considered "unfair to the author" in being "nothing but a
warped summary" and "dangerous" as "a bad piece of
work . . . sponsored by a magazine of The Dial's reputation." Almost simultaneously with the complaint we received a letter from the ill-treated author, who said in conclusion, "And may I tell you how much I was pleased with
A. A. A.'s review of ———— ———? Quite apart from the fact that
it was kind, it seemed to me an almost miraculous 'sum-
ming-up.' I have always wondered if A. A. A. was a nom de
plume. Will you extend my thanks to him or her?"

Occasional inadvertences, moreover, at the expense of the
acting editor, were not wanting—sundry inquiries request-
ing the attention of the "Active Editor"; a letter from one
of our Spanish contributors beginning, "My respectable
Miss"; and, resulting from statements about The Dial
Award as acknowledging a contribution to "letters," offers
to provide any sort of letters we required.

It was an office truism that a manuscript returned with
a printed card had been read as carefully as manuscript returned with a letter. But occasionally there was the compliment of anger, from those whose grievances were imaginary
as from those whose grudges were real. Some were so in-

curious in their reading as to accuse us of anti-Semitism, or hid salt between pages to test the intensiveness of our reading. But not all "contributors who were not allowed to contribute" bit the hand that had not fed them. One to whom Alyse Gregory had given advice replied that before submitting work to *The Dial* he had not known there was such a thing as editorial reciprocity, that he had rejection slips enough "to paper the Washington Monument inside and out"; that at last, however, as the result of *The Dial's* encouragement, he was appearing regularly in the XYZ (a fiction magazine of robust circulation). And I recall the generous disappointment of a writer whose work had elicited suggestions, when we returned to him a check that he had thought might be "used for a reckless meal."

Misunderstandings were with us in most instances, like skepticism that "doubts in order to believe"; and anything in the way of ill-wishing fulminations was constantly neutralized by over-justice from other quarters; by such stringence against encroachment as Raymond Mortimer's, when he wondered if certain requested work might not be done more to our liking by someone else, and by his patience when *Dial* work of his was reprinted without his permission; by Gilbert Seldes' magnanimity toward a minor phase of collaboration, and L. A. G. Strong's willingness to believe that editorial crotchets are not all of the devil; by Yvor Winters' conscientious resistances and tincture of editorial virus; by such quixotry as Professor Saintsbury's hesitating to incorporate in an article on Poe material that Andrew Lang had not published, saying that once an article had been declined, he did not care to offer it "to the most different of editors"; by Professor Charles Sears Baldwin's acquiescent addendum in omitting a touch of underlining humor, "You are not only good friends but good critics."

To some contributors—as to some non-contributors—*The Dial*, and I in particular, may have seemed quarrelsome, and it is regrettable that manners should be subordinated to matter. Mishaps and anomalies, however, but served to emphasize for me the untoxic soundness of most writers. And today, previous victims of mine have to dread from me, as pre-empting the privilege of the last word, nothing more than solicitude that all of us may write better.

I think of Mr. McBride—his punctuality and his punctuation, each comma placed with unaccidental permanence, and the comfortable equability of his pitiless ultimatums. One does not lose that sense of "creeping up on the French," of music, of poetry, of fiction, of society sparkle, that came with his visits to the office. He did not "specialize in frights," nor in defamation, nor nurse grudges; and too reverent to speak in religious accents often, could not trust himself to dwell on personal losses, sentiment with him was so intense.

Gaston Lachaise's stubbornness and naturalness were a work of art above even the most important sculpture. Admitting to an undiminishing sense of burden that made frivolities or time-killings a sort of poison to him, he was as deliberate as if under a spell. I remember his saying with almost primitive-tribal moroseness, "But I believe in a large amount of work"; as on another occasion, "Cats. I could learn a million of things from cats." And there was, *when* there was, E. E. Cummings, the really successful avoider of compromise, of scarecrow insincerity, of rubber-stamp hundred-per-cent deadness.

I think of Charles Sheeler coping with the difficulty of
photographing for reproduction Lachaise's polished brass
head of Scofield Thayer, mounted on glass—glitteringly
complicated from any angle—and have never seen anything effected with less ado or greater care; these scientif-
ically businesslike proceedings reminding one of the wonderfully mastered Bucks County barn and winding stair
turn.

Decorum, generosity, and genially decorative improve-
ments to the proofsheets were matched in Gordon Craig by
an unsubservience justifying the surname "crag" as synonym
for Craig. I recall Ezra Pound's precision as translator of
Boris de Schloezer—reinforced by an almost horrendous
explicitness on returned proofs. But nothing supplants in
recollection the undozing linguistics and scholarly resource-
fulness of Ellen Thayer as assistant editor; occasional un-
tender accusations from authors, of stupidity or neglect of
revisions, being found invariably to be reversible.

Padraic Colum's clemency and afflatus were not confined
to the printed page, and upon his visits to the office, routine
atmosphere was transformed into one of discovery. And
John Cowper Powys, inalienable verbalist and student of
strangeness, inventor of the term "fairy cardinal" for Padraic
Colum, seemed himself a supernatural being; so good a
Samaritan, any other phase of endowment was almost an
overplus. As Mrs. Watson said of his conversation, "He is so
intense, you don't know whether he's talking or listening."
And his brother Llewelyn's dislike of "a naturalist with an
umbrella," of shams and pickthank science, come back to
one in connection with his gift for metaphor; also, to one
who has known the shallows of a tree-bordered stream, his

phrase, "the cider-coloured reaches of The Stour." And though suicidally kind to victims of injustice, he was as aloof from the world of non-books as a fish without eyes.

Above all, for an inflexible morality against "the nearly good"; for a non-exploiting helpfulness to art and the artist, for living the doctrine that "a love of letters knows no frontiers," Scofield Thayer and Dr. Watson are the indestructible symbol. One recalls their support of James Joyce when *The Little Review* was censored for publishing *Ulysses*. "Our insistence that *The Dial*'s award is not a prize is frequently taken to be a characteristic pedantry on our part," they said, but "a prize is something competed for, an award is given—given to afford the recipient an opportunity to do what he wishes and out of that to enrich and develop his work." Nor was a gift ever more complete and without victimizing involvements.

As it was Abraham Lincoln's ideal to lift "artificial weights from all shoulders . . . and afford all an unfettered start," so here. And since in lifting weights money has its part, contributions were paid for on acceptance; for prose, two cents a word; for verse, twenty dollars a page or part of a page; for reviews termed Briefer Mentions, two dollars each. There were not special prices for special contributors —a phase of chivalry toward beginners that certain of them suspiciously disbelieved in. Any writing or translating by the editors was done without payment, Dr. Watson's participation, under the name W. C. Blum, being contrived with "quietness amounting to scandal." And payment was computed in amounts that are multiples of five. For example, as stated in our manual of procedure: "If a manuscript counts up to $15.98 or $16.01 or $18.01, the writer should be paid $20.00; and if same is more than $90.00 it should be computed in multiples of ten."

Writing is an undertaking for the modest. Those of us employed at *The Dial* felt that the devisers of the organization we represented could do better than we what we were trying to do, and we shall ever feel their strength of purpose toward straightness, spontaneity, and usefulness. "If," as has been said, "*The Dial* had rough seas to navigate because it chose to sail uncharted zones, structure was the better tested"; and I think happily of the days when I was part of it.

SIR FRANCIS BACON[1]

In his *Studies of Extraordinary Prose,* Lafcadio Hearn
says, "You cannot appeal to the largest possible audience
with a scholarly style." This would seem to be true; but expressions of deep conviction, in all ages, weather coldness,
and Sir Francis Bacon's "exact diligence" and pleasing defiances anticipated not only the mind of close successors, but of
our own age. "There is no excellent beauty that hath not
strangeness in the proportion" recalls Burke's statement, in
his essay "On the Sublime and the Beautiful," that beauty
is striking as deformity is striking—in its novelty; also
Ruskin's summary of beauty as beauty of behavior affirms the
statement, "No youth can be comely but by pardon and
considering the youth." When Bacon says of masques that
the eye must be relieved "before it be full of the same object," since "it is a great pleasure to desire to see that it
cannot perfectly discern," one is reminded of Santayana's
observation that "nothing absorbs the consciousness so
much as what is not quite given."

There is a renovating quality in the work of early writers,
as also in so-called "broken" speech in which we have the
idiom of one language in the words of another. Sir Francis
Bacon surely has this raciness, as when he says, "I have
marvelled sometimes at Spain how they clasp and contain
so large dominions with so few natural Spaniards," and de-

1 *The Dial,* April 1924.

fines moss as "a rudiment between putrefaction and an herb"; the vigor of the writer's nature being, of course, the key to his "efficacy," as when he says of anger, "To seek to extinguish anger utterly is but a bravery of the Stoics. We have better oracles"; and what of, "A civil war is like the heat of fever but a foreign war is like the heat of exercise"? In Sir Francis Bacon, conclusiveness and contempt for tact are always at variance with caution, his desire for efficiency pertaining even to death: "I would out of a care to do the best business well, ever keep a guard, and stand upon keeping faith with a good conscience. And I would die together, and not my mind often, my body once."

His insight into human idiosyncrasy has a flavor of Machiavelli, as when he says, "I knew one that when he wrote a letter, he would put that which was most material in the postscript as it had been a bye matter"; of boldness, "It doth fascinate and bind hand and foot, those that are shallow in judgment and weak in courage, and prevaileth with wise men at weak times." Of blindness to one's own defects, he remarks that there is a confidence "like as we shall see it commonly in poets, that if they show their verses and you except to any, they will say that that line cost them more labour than all the rest." Of pulling down the ambitious, he says, "The only way is the interchange continually of favours and disgraces, whereby they may not know what to expect and be as it were in a wood." "As for jest, there be certain things which ought to be privileged from it," he says. "Men ought to find the difference between saltness and bitterness. Certainly, he that hath a satirical vein, as he maketh others afraid of his wit, so need he be afraid of others' memory."

Bacon admires Machiavelli's suiting of form to matter; he feels letters to be an "even more particular representation of business" than "chronicles or lives"; and says those who have returned to Caesar's *Commentaries* after a first compulsory reading will perhaps agree that in "Caesar's history, entitled only a commentary," there are solid weight of matter, real passages, and lively images of actions and persons, expressed in the greatest propriety of words and perspicuity of narration that ever was." Moreover, his differentiation of poetry from prose is entertaining. Poetry, he says, has "more unexpected and alternative variation," and in "being not tied to the laws of nature, may at pleasure join that which nature has severed and sever that which nature hath joined."

A student of human nature and of words ought to be able to tell a story, and Bacon winds quickly into the heart of an episode—in *The New Atlantis*; in the essays, as when he says, "It is sport to see when a bold fellow is out of countenance, at a stay like a stale at chess"; and in *The Advancement of Learning*, in the account of Xenophon's prowess and Falinus's skepticism: " 'If I be not deceived, young gentleman, you are an Athenian and I believe you study philosophy and it is pretty that you say, but you are much abused if you think your virtue can stand the king's power.' Here was the scorn," says Bacon. "The wonder followed." Not only as he exposits mythology in *The Wisdom of the Ancients* but as narrator of facts in *The History of Henry VII*, he is a siren of ingenuity. The circumstantial manner of a novel continually refreshes the content, as when the queen's coronation is likened to a christening that has been put off until the child is old enough to walk to the altar; and exact without being labored, Bacon says the king "was a comely personage, a little above just stature, well and straight limbed but slender. His countenance was reverend, and a little like a churchman. But it was to the disadvantage of the painter for it was best when he spake." Could anything be more chiseled than the closing sentences of this history? "He was born at Pembroke Castle, and lieth buried at Westminster, in one of the stateliest and daintiest monuments of Europe, both for the chapel and the sepulchre. So that he dwelleth more richly dead, in the monument of his tomb, than he did alive in Richmond or any of his palaces."

The essays have perhaps absorbed interest which belongs to the other writings and have stood as a barrier to the daring of the other. The aphorisms and allusions to antiquity have an effect of formula; quoted wisdom from Greek, Roman, Hebrew, and Italian sages tending to excuse attention as much as to concentrate it. One thinks of the early essays in relation to the *History of Henry VII* somewhat as one thinks of an anthology in relation to a novel. "Even in divinity," Bacon says, "some writings have more of the eagle than others"; and in *The Advancement of Learning* there is conspicuously much of the eagle. It is understandable that Bacon should say, "If the first reading will make an objection, the second will make an answer."

BESITZ UND GEMEINGUT[1]

DR. BRANDES has in this biography remembered what Goethe counsels the biographer not to forget—that succeeding generations have a flimsy idea of preceding periods; that nothing is to be assumed, everything is to be related. We should, however, welcome a consideration of *Dichtung and Wahrheit* fuller than the slender chapter which Dr. Brandes vouchsafes us, and are defrauded in the absence of any but cursory allusions to Goethe's letters, essays, and reviews. Furthermore, one feels Dr. Brandes to be a more "trusting" student of Goethe than one is oneself when he says that "by the mere touch of his spiritual personality Goethe had initiated Carlyle into life and literature"; that in "publishing under his own name the most beautiful poems Marianne von Willemer ever produced," he "conferred honor when he took." Dr. Brandes's gift of epithet is manifest in his alluding to Bettina's "burrlike hanging on" and "youthful boldness," to Schiller's "noble and striving nature"; in his characterizing Frau von Klettenberg as "a Protestant nun" and Goethe as "a fortress, not an open town"; his military pre-empting of judgment, however, would scarcely convert one to his admiration for Goethe if one did not already share it. A certain infelicity of speech is heightened, one suspects, by the translation, in which, notwithstanding the translator's confessed loyalty

[1] Review of Georg Brandes's *Wolfgang Goethe*, in *The Dial*, June 1925.

to the text, his idea of idiom seems a false one, resulting as it does in such phrases as "quite a few," "quite a while," "measured up," "forever and a day," "apt to be full of," and "time out of mind."

That of which one is above all, and always delightfully, conscious throughout the work is Goethe's lyric power, especially valuing what is said of his "musical skill" and "tonal depth"—as a result of which greater effects have "never been produced by fewer words and simpler means." Although certain poems quoted by Dr. Brandes do not seem to us "immortal masterpieces," we feel "the fire," "the manly seriousness," "the tenderness," "the real humor," "the great glamour," the "inner richness of Goethe's being, which makes it impossible for even a short stanza to be empty."

We are especially indebted to Dr. Brandes for his paragraphs upon Goethe as counsel for the defense in certain legal cases and for his comment upon Goethe's discoveries in anatomy, geology, and botany, for which, he says, "we feel a respect nearly deeper than that evoked by his purely poetic creations."

"Casting off works in the process of self-creation," describing his life as "the incessant turning and lifting of a stone that had to be turned and lifted once more," Goethe is himself, as Dr. Brandes implies, his greatest work of art. This man who "never rode on a railway train, never sailed on a steamship, who read by a tallow lamp and wrote with a goosequill," who "never saw Paris, never saw London, never saw St. Petersburg, never saw Vienna," and caught but a fleeting glimpse of Berlin, "was within himself a whole and complete civilization." "He was among minds," as Dr. Brandes says, "what the Pacific Ocean is among the waters of the earth. In reality only a small part of it is pacific." We see an evolving enthusiasm in which a preference for Gothic is "wheeled about" to a preference for the art of ancient Greece, "somewhat as one would turn a fiery charger." Aloof from politics, yet as a passionate economist he appears "in the person of the singular uncle in *Wilhelm Meisters Wanderjahre*, whose watchword, '*Besitz und Gemeingut*,' was inscribed round about on his various buildings somewhat as the Oriental peoples adorn the walls of their houses with excerpts from the Koran." We see his spiritual independence, his love of liberty as "the opposite of coercion, but not the opposite of a voluntary subjection to such coercion as that of moral discipline, or that of metrics, or social forms, or reasonable law"—a concept embodied in his saying, "*Und das Gesetz nur kann uns Freiheit geben.*" We recall with Croce his "opposing that in French literature which was intellectualistic and ironical, aged and correct like an old lady," as against his reviling "those Germans who were wont to justify every unseemliness they wrote by saying that they had 'lived it.'" We see his inconquerably social nature, as evinced by his many friends; a distrust of his age, on the other hand, such that "when finally as a result of extraordinary exertion he had finished the second part of *Faust,* he sealed the manuscript with seven seals and laid it aside for posterity, convinced that his contemporaries would simply misunderstand it." By this "development of the soul in accord with its inborn ability," we are reminded of "that manifoldness in simplicity of mountains" which Goethe himself admired.

O F T H E S E essays and papers by George Saintsbury, two
have not before been printed. In all, there is "the old gay
pugnacity" of one not thus far "disabled"; and an im-
penitent Toryism so opposed in every nerve to "the washy
semi-Socialism, half sentimental, half servile, which is the
governing spirit of all but a few politicians today," that it
would seem in its own right to exemplify "that single-
hearted and single-minded insanity of genius which carries
a movement completely to its goal."

We feel it is the novelist speaking, as well as the critic,
in the biographical summaries and paraphrases of plot; in
the statement that Xenophon's *Cyropaedia* "is a philosoph-
ical romance for which its author has chosen to borrow a
historic name or two"; and that one critic at least has an
acute understanding of "the very important division of
human sentiment, which is called for shortness, love." What
relish for life there is in this elaborating of the Ettrick
Shepherd's statement that "A' contributors are in a manner
fierce." "The contributor who is not allowed to contribute,"
says Mr. Saintsbury, "is fierce, as a matter of course; but
not less fierce is the contributor who thinks himself too

[1] Review of *The Collected Essays and Papers of George Saintsbury*, 1875–
1920, in *The Dial*, October 1925.

much edited, and the contributor who imperatively insists that his article on Chinese metaphysics shall go in at once, and the contributor who, being an excellent hand at the currency, wants to be allowed to write on dancing; and, in short, as the Shepherd says, all contributors."

It is Mr. Saintsbury's conviction that "the greatest part, if not the whole of the pleasure-giving appeal of poetry, lies in its sound rather than in its sense"—that "no 'chain of extremely valuable thoughts' is poetry in itself." Objections suggest themselves, and one can understand the comment on Matthew Arnold: "I cannot quite make out why the critic did not say to the poet, 'It will never do to publish verse like this and this and this and this,' or why the poet did not say to the critic, 'Then we will make it worth publishing,' and proceed to do so."

Despite trifling divergence from impartiality in the appeal to "any fit reader," to "any competent judge," to "any tolerably intelligent critic," one cannot fail to be exhilarated in these pages by its ever-present equity, as in the statement, "It will be only in a way for [a man's] greater glory if you find out where and wherefore he is sometimes wrong." Essentially "a thoughtful person" in the desire to give facts "without violating the sanctity of private life," Mr. Saintsbury admits that he "may have 'most politely, most politely' made some authors uncomfortable," but reminds one that, to reviewers, "Stiletto and pole-axe, sandbag and scavenger-shovel, are barred"—that one "can administer sequins as well as lashes, and send a man to ride round the town in royal apparel as well as despatch him to the gallows."

The work vibrates with contempt for "twentieth-hand learning"—is alive with a voracity that has "grappled with

whole libraries." "I have seen disdainful remarks," says Mr.
Saintsbury, "on those critics who, however warily, admire
a considerable number of authors, as though they were
coarse and omnivorous persons. . . . A man need not be a
Don Juan of letters to have a list of almost *mille e tre* loves
in that department." The impassioned temper of these
essays is in itself a pleasure, as when we have Macaulay
"not only 'cocksure' but cock-a-hoop," and "the average
mid-century Liberal" regarding Carlyle as "a man whose
dearest delight it was to gore and toss and trample the
sweetest and most sacred principles of the Manchester
School." Mr. Saintsbury recalls to us "the massive common
sense and nervous diction" of Dryden, whom he denom-
inates "a poetical schoolman"; "the extraordinary command
of metre which led Swinburne to plan sea-serpents in verse
in order to show how easily and gracefully he can make
them coil and uncoil their enormous length"; and says of Mr.
Scarborough's family, in connection with Trollope's "economy and yet opulence of material," "If you have any sense
of the particular art you can't help feeling the skill with
which the artist wheels you along till he feels inclined to
turn you out of his barrow and then deposits you at his if
not your destination."

One does not correct the speech of those who make our
speech correct, but Mr. Saintsbury's "Heaven knows" seems
a needless superlative on completeness. "With the im-
periousness natural to all art," however, "style absolutely
refuses to avail itself of, or to be found in, company with
anything that is ready made," and as might be expected
in the work of one who has written a *History of English
Prosody*, we have here a style in which there is often "a

perfection of expression which transmutes the subject"; a security which can say, "There is no wing in Crabbe, there is no transport." These essays have wing, a grace that recalls the Bible, Cicero, the seventeenth century, and "the engaging idiom of the Gaul."

Referring to Carlyle's life of Sterling, Mr. Saintsbury says, "I have seldom been able to begin it again or even to consult it for a casual reference, without following it right through." So with any piece of writing by George Saintsbury, one must follow it through, grateful forever to the essays on Lockhart, "Some Great Biographies," to those on the grand style, on Macaulay, "Bolshevism in Its Cradle," and to "The Life and Opinions of William Godwin."

ICHOR OF IMAGINATION [1]

I N *The Infernal Machine,* Jean Cocteau is as he was in *Orphée,* a " 'fantaisiste' on a known theme." Fulfilling the prediction of the oracle, as in Sophocles, Oedipus kills his father Laius (by accident, not knowing the victim), thwarts the Sphinx (the devourer of the young men of Thebes), is rewarded by marriage with Jocasta (the queen, his own unrecognized mother), and, having been made aware of his guilt, puts out his own eyes. "He solves riddles, becomes king and an object of affection, is envied of all, yet suffers a desperate end; never call a man happy until you have read the last chapter" is the summary by Sophocles, and with it one compares *The Infernal Machine* by Cocteau, also Carl Wildman's statement in the introduction: Cocteau "has dived with the greatest ease into the heart of the legend and brought back the almost sacred characters stiff with glory, brought them back to life, humanized them." Act I lacks contagion, but the play does gradually compel in the reader an author-forgotten, participating suspense.

A potent device in fiction or drama is that in which one character describes another to that other, unaware that he addresses the person of whom he speaks. Of this principle, inherent in the original *Oedipus,* Cocteau has made the most; as in Jocasta's remark, "What a courteous young man! He must have been taken care of by a very kind

---

[1] Review of Jean Cocteau's *The Infernal Machine* (Introduction and English Version by Carl Wildman), in *The Nation,* February 6, 1937.

126

mother, very kind"; and where, misconceiving the recoil of awareness with which Jocasta recognizes scars on his feet, Oedipus says they were "from the hunt, I think." This principle is extended by Cocteau in the encounter of the Theban matron with the young girl in white, whom she warns against the Sphinx. Sophocles' device of the corroborating shepherd who confirms Oedipus to himself is matched by Cocteau in the episode of the talisman returned to Oedipus by Teresias—the belt Oedipus had given the Sphinx, saying, "This will bring you to me when I have killed the beast." It is a good moment in Act I in which Laius's ghost calls to Jocasta and the soldiers—undiscerned by them while they commiserate with one another on its non-appearing; and there is drama in the mockery of Oedipus by Anubis, in the nightmare—Anubis repeating the words Oedipus had naïvely spoken to the Sphinx, "Thanks to my unhappy childhood . . ."

"Logic forces us to appear to men in the shape in which they imagine us; otherwise they would see only emptiness," Anubis is made to say—a statement of which the invisible ghost of Laius is an illustration; also a clue to the mind of Jean Cocteau himself. The extra character, Anubis—death's orderly—is an invention especially characteristic of Cocteau—cognate to Azrael and Raphael, death's assistants in *Orphée*, in which play "darkness has been shown in broad daylight," Mr. Wildman says. And always it is as the poet we must think of Cocteau—the person who says, "a thing can rarely at the same time be and seem true," who says he is "incapable of writing a play for or against anything"; and warns one that "it is not the poet's role to produce cumbersome proofs." M. Cocteau does not spread his cloak on the mud, he does not make promises, and his temperament permeates all his concepts; he is fervent. His ardor, voracity of presentment, inexhaustible fund of metaphor, and fastidious apperceptiveness seem rivaled only by that of the animals.

Aphorism is one of the kindlier phases of poetic autocracy —used from time to time in *The Infernal Machine*. Creon says, "The most secret of secrets are betrayed one day or another to the determined seeker," and the Soldier says, "A word of advice: let princes deal with princes, phantoms with phantoms, and soldiers with soldiers." But going beyond mere incisiveness, M. Cocteau sometimes imparts to a word a lovable neatness, such as we have in Aristophanes, where he speaks of the man who whiled away the time making frogs from fruit skins. We have it in Corbière and in E. E. Cummings; and in Clarence Day, where "L'hippopotame" is introduced as the Biblical behemoth.

Cocteau's vituperative tendency toward contentiousness appears in the Soldier's banter; and, as Mr. Wildman notes, in the Sphinx. Still more marked—as an asset, however— is the tendency to incantation. One sees it in Le Grand Ecart, in the Narcissus passage, where the river "cares nothing about the nymphs or the trees it reflects—longing only for the sea"; and in the Sphinx's self-characterization: "A judge is not so unalterable, an insect so voracious, a bird so carnivorous, the egg so nocturnal, a Chinese executioner so ingenious, the heart so unpredictable, the prestidigitator so deft, the star so portentous, the snake sliming its prey so intent . . . I speak, I work, I wind, I unwind, I calculate, I muse, I weave, I winnow, I knit, I plait. . . ."

The author has invested the play with modern emotion

and, reveling in verisimilitude, causes Jocasta to say to
Oedipus as she lifts him from the nightmare, "Don't make
yourself heavy, help me." Oedipus, vivid and panting, arrests the eye, Jocasta half infatuates, the Sphinx—symboliz-
ing the machinery of the gods' injustice—inspires fear,
though her femininity and emphasized claws point to a cro-
chet on M. Cocteau's part. He appears to have an unfemi-
nist yet not wholly detached attitude to woman; Jocasta
being, like the Sphinx, "of the sex disturbing to heroes."
Burdensome yet seductive, she asks, "Am I so old then?"
and adds, "Women say things to be contradicted. They always hope it isn't true."

At the end of the play, instead of a somber dimming of
personality, as in the Greek, there is an allusion to "glory,"
as completing the destiny of Oedipus. *Ought* horror to
be believed?

Aware that imagination with Jean Cocteau is no appurtenance but an ichor, as it was shown to be in *Le Sang d'un
Poète*, one has, nevertheless, the sense of something submerged and estranged, of a somnambulist with feet tied, of
a musical instrument in a museum, that should be sounding;
of valor in a fairy tale, changed by hostile enchantment into
a frog or a carp that cannot leave its pool or well. In myth
there is a principle of penalty: Snow White must not open
the door of the dwarfs' house when the peddler knocks,
Pandora must not open the box, Perseus must not look at
the Gorgon except in his shield; and M. Cocteau, in refusing to be answerable to any morality but his own, is in the
Greek sense impious and unnatural. But he is a very fine
inhabitant of the world in which ichor is imagination, in
which magic imparts itself to whatever he writes.

COMPACTNESS COMPACTED[1]

W O M E N are not noted for terseness, but Louise Bogan's art is compactness compacted. Emotion with her, as she has said of certain fiction, is "itself form, the kernel which builds outward form from inward intensity." She uses a kind of forged rhetoric that nevertheless seems inevitable. It is almost formula with her to omit the instinctive comma of self-defensive explanation, for example, "Our lives through we have trod the ground." Her titles are right poetically, with no subserviences for torpid minds to catch at; the lines entitled "Knowledge," for instance, being really about love. And there is fire in the brazier—the thinker in the poet. "Fifteenth Farewell" says:

> I erred, when I thought loneliness the wide
> Scent of mown grass over forsaken fields,
> Or any shadow isolation yields.
> Loneliness was the heart within your side.

One is struck by her restraint—an unusual courtesy in this day of bombast. The triumph of what purports to be surrender, in the "Poem in Prose," should be studied entire.

Miss Bogan is a workman, in prose or in verse. Anodynes are intolerable to her. She refuses to be deceived or self-deceived. Her work is not mannered. There are in it thoughts

[1] Review of Louise Bogan's *Poems and New Poems,* in *The Nation,* November 15, 1941.

130

about the disunities of "the single mirrored against the single," about the devouring gorgon romantic love, toward which, as toward wine, unfaith is renewal; thoughts about the solace and futilities of being brave; about the mind as a refuge—"crafty knight" that is itself "Prey to an end not evident to craft"; about grudges; about no longer treating memory "as rich stuff . . . in a cedarn dark, . . . as eggs under the wings," but as

> Rubble in gardens, it and stones alike,
> That any spade may strike.

We read of "The hate that bruises, though the heart is braced"; of "one note rage can understand"; of "chastity's futility" and "pain's effrontery"; of "memory's false measure." No Uncle Remus phase of nature, this about the crows and the woman whose prototype is the briar patch: "She is a stem long hardened./A weed that no scythe mows." Could the uninsisted-on surgery of exposition be stricter than in the term "red" for winter grass, or evoke the contorted furor of flame better than by saying the fire ceased its "thresh"? We have "The lilac like a heart" (preceded by the word "leaves"); "See now the stretched hawk fly"; "Horses in half-ploughed fields/Make earth they walk upon a changing color." Most delicate of all,

> . . . we heard the cock
> Shout its unplaceable cry, the axe's sound
> Delay a moment after the axe's stroke.

Music here is not someone's idol, but experience. There are real rhymes, the rhyme with vowel cognates, and consonant resonances so perfect one is not inclined to wonder whether the sound is a vowel or a consonant—as in "The Crossed Apple":

> . . . this side is red without a dapple,
> And this side's hue
> Is clear and snowy. It's a lovely apple.
> It is for you.

In "fed with fire" we have expert use of the enhancing exception to the end-stopped line:

> And spiny fruits up through the earth are fed
> With fire;

Best of all is the embodied climax with unforced subsiding cadence, as in the song about

> The stone—the deaf, the blind—
> That sees the birds in flock
> Steer narrowed to the wind.

When a tune plagues the ear, the best way to be rid of it is to let it forth unhindered. This Miss Bogan has done with a W. H. Auden progression, "Evening in the Sanitarium"; with G. M. Hopkins in "Feuer-Nacht"; Ezra Pound in "The Sleeping Fury"; W. B. Yeats in "Betrothed"; W. C. Williams in "Zone." All through, there is a certain residual, securely equated seventeenth-century firmness, as in the spectacular competence of Animal, Vegetable, and Mineral.

What of the implications? For mortal rage and immortal injury, are there or are there not medicines? Job and Hamlet insisted that we dare not let ourselves be snared into hating hatefulness; to do this would be to take our own lives. Harmed, let us say, through our generosity—if we consent to have pity on our illusions and others' absence of illusion, to condone the fact that "no fine body ever can be meat and drink to anyone"—is it true that pain will exchange its role and become servant instead of master? Or is it merely a conveniently unexpunged superstition?

Those who have seemed to know most about eternity feel that this side of eternity is a small part of life. We are told, if we do wrong that grace may abound, it does not abound. We need not be told that life is never going to be free from trouble and that there are no substitutes for the dead; but it is a fact as well as a mystery that weakness is power, that handicap is proficiency, that the scar is a credential, that indignation is no adversary for gratitude, or heroism for joy. There are medicines.

THE DIAL *Award* [1]

WILLIAM CARLOS WILLIAMS is a physician, a resident of New Jersey, the author of prose and verse. He has written of "fences and outhouses built of barrel-staves and parts of boxes," of the "sparkling lady" who "passes quickly to the seclusion of her carriage," of Weehawken, of "The Passaic, that filthy river," of "hawsers that drop and groan," of "a young horse with a green bed-quilt on his withers." His "venomous accuracy," if we may use the words used by him in speaking of the author of "The Raven," is opposed to "makeshifts, self-deceptions and grotesque excuses." Among his meditations are chickory and daisies, Queen Anne's lace, trees—hairy, bent, erect—orchids and magnolias. We need not, as Wallace Stevens has said, "try to . . . evolve a mainland from his leaves, scents and floating bottles and boxes." "What Columbus discovered is nothing

[1] *The Dial*, January 1927, commenting on *The Dial* Award for 1926 to Dr. Williams. The announcement of the Award by Scofield Thayer and J. S. Watson read in part as follows: "*The Dial's* award 'crowns' no book. . . . It indicates only that the recipient has done a service to letters and that, since money is required even by those who serve letters, since the payment in money is generally so inadequate when good work is concerned, *The Dial* is in a way adding to the earnings of a writer, diminishing, by a little, the discrepancy between his minimum requirements as a citzien in a commercial society and his earnings as an artist."

to what Williams is looking for." He writes of lions with Ashurbanipal's "shafts bristling in their necks," of "the bare backyard of the old Negro with white hair," of "branches that have lain in a fog which now a wind is blowing away." "This modest quality of realness, which he attributes to 'contact' with the good Jersey dirt, sometimes reminds one of Chekhov," a connoisseur of our poetry says. "Like Chekhov, he knows animals and babies as well as trees. And to people who are looking for the story, his poems must often seem as disconnected and centrifugal as Chekhov's later plays." We agree that "his phrases have a simplicity, a solid justice." He "is forthright, a hard, straight, bitter javelin," William Marion Reedy said.

A child is a "portent"; a poet is a portent. As has been said of certain theological architecture, it is the peculiarity of certain poetic architecture that "the foundations are ingeniously supported by the superstructure." The child

> Sleeps fast till his might
>   Shall be piled
> Sinew on sinew.

In imagination's arboreal world of thought, as in the material world,

> creeping energy, concentrated
> counterforce—welds sky, buds, trees.

As said, William Carlos Williams is a doctor. Physicians are not so often poets as poets are physicians, but may we not assert that oppositions of science are not oppositions to poetry but oppositions to falseness? The author of the *Religio Medici*—not more a physician than poet—"has many *verba ardentia*," Dr. Johnson observed, "forcible expressions which he would never have found, but by venturing to the utmost verge of propriety; and flights which would never have been reached, but by one who had very little fear of the shame of falling."

In one of Dr. Williams' books we find a poem entitled, "To Wish Courage to Myself." It is to wish courage to him and, in the inviting of his hardy spirit, to wish it to ourselves that we have—inadequately—spoken.

"Things Others Never Notice" [1]

S T R U G G L E is a main force in William Carlos Williams. And the breathless budding of thought from thought is one of the results and charms of the pressure configured. With an abandon born of inner security, Dr. Williams somewhere nicknames his chains of incontrovertibly logical apparent non-sequiturs, rigmarole; and a consciousness of life and intrepidity is characteristically present in "Stop: Go—"

> a green truck
> dragging a concrete mixer
> passes
> in the street—
> the clatter and true sound
> of verse—

Disliking the tawdriness of unnecessary explanation, the detracting compulsory connective, stock speech of any kind,

[1] Review of William Carlos Williams' *Collected Poems*, *1921–1931*, with Preface by Wallace Stevens, in *Poetry*, May 1934.

he sets the words down, "each note secure in its own posture—singularly woven." "The senseless unarrangement of wild things," which he imitates, makes some kinds of correct writing look rather foolish; and as illustrating that combination of energy and composure which is the expertness of the artist, he has never drawn a clearer self-portrait than "Birds and Flowers":

> What have I done
> to drive you away? It is
> winter, true enough, but
>
> this day I love you.
> This day
> there is no time at all
>
> more than in under
> my ribs where anatomists
> say the heart is—
>
> And just today you
> will not have me. Well,
> tomorrow it may be snowing—
>
> I'll keep after you, your
> repulse of me is no more
> than a rebuff to the weather—
>
> If we make a desert of
> ourselves—we make
> a desert . . .

William Carlos Williams objects to urbanity—to sleek and natty effects—and this is a good sign if not always a good thing. Yet usually nothing could better the dashing shrewdness of the pattern as he develops it and cuts it off at the acutely right point.

With the bee's sense of polarity he searches for a flower, and that flower is representation. Likenesses here are not reminders of the object, they are it, as in "Struggle of Wings":

> And there's the river with thin ice upon it
> fanning out half over the black
> water, the free middlewater racing under its
> ripples that move crosswise on the stream.

He is drugged with romance—"O unlit candle with the soft white plume"—but, like the bee, is neither a waif nor a fool. Argus-eyed, energetic, insatiate, compassionate, undeceived, he says in "Immortal,"

> Yes, there is one thing braver than all flowers;
>
> .   .   .
>
> And thy name, lovely One, is Ignorance.

Wide-eyed resignation of this kind helps some to be cynical, but it makes Dr. Williams considerate; sorry for the tethered bull, the circus sea-elephant, for the organ-grinder, "sour-faced," "needing a shave."

He ponders "the justice of poverty/its shame, its dirt" and pities the artist's hindered energy as it patiently does what it ought to do, and the poem read by critics who have no inkling of what it's about. But the pathos is incidental. The "ability to be drunk with a sudden realization of value in things others never notice" can metamorphose our detestable reasonableness and offset a whole planetary system of deadness. "The burning liquor of the moonlight" makes provable things mild by comparison. The poem often is about nothing that we wish to give our attention to, but if it is something he wishes our attention for, what is urgent for him becomes urgent for us. His uncompromising conscientiousness sometimes seems misplaced; he is at times almost insultingly specific, but there is in him—and this must be our consolation—that dissatisfied expanding energy, the emotion, the *ergo* of the medieval dialectician, the "therefore" which is the distinguishing mark of the artist.

Various poems that are not here again suggest the bee— and a too eclectic disposing of the honey.

Dr. Williams does not compromise, and Wallace Stevens is another resister whose way of saying what he says is as important as what is said. Mr. Stevens' presentation of the book refreshes a grievance—the scarcity of prose about verse from him, one of the few persons who should have something to say. But poetry in America has not died, so long as these two "young sycamores" are able to stand the winters that we have, and the inhabitants.

"ONE'S not half two. Its two are halves of one": Mr. Cummings says. So 1 × 1 is a merging of two things in a "sunlight of oneness," "one thou"; and "beginning a whole verbal adventure," this onederful book is primarily a compliment to friendship.

It is a book of wisdom that knowledge cannot contradict; of mind that is heart because it is alive; of wealth that is nothing but joy. Its axioms are also inventions: "as yes is to if, love is to yes," for instance; and

> all ignorance toboggans into know
> and trudges up to ignorance again:

Ignorance that has become know is to Mr. Cummings a monster; and nothing could say how valuable he is in slaying this "collective pseudobeast" in its

> . . . scienti
> fic land of supernod
> where freedom is compulsory
> and only man is god

It is useless to search in a book by E. E. Cummings for explanations, reasons, becauses, dead words, or dead ways. His poems, furthermore, are not encumbered with punctuation; you are expected to feel the commas and the periods. The dislocating of letters that are usually conjoined in a

[1] Review of E. E. Cummings' 1 × 1, in *The Nation*, April 1, 1944.

140

syllable or word is not a madness of the printer but impassioned feeling that hazards its life for the sake of emphasis.
For E. E. Cummings, the parts of speech are living creatures
that alter and grow. Disliking “all dull nouns,” he concocts
new ones that are phenomena of courage and mobility.
Nouns become adjectives; and adverbs, adjectives. His hero
and heroine are “mythical guests of Is”; truth is “where-
less,” and “ there’s nothing as something as one.”

“I am abnormally fond of that precision which creates
movement,” he says, and we see how a sensibility of crystal-
line explicitness can achieve, without using the word, a poem
about a kite and have it resplendent art:

> o by the by
> has anybody seen
> little you-i
> who stood on a green
> hill and threw
> his wish at blue
>
> with a swoop and a dart
> out flew his wish
> (it dived like a fish
> but climbed like a dream)
> throbbing like a heart
> singing like a flame
>
> blue took it my
> far beyond far
> and high beyond high
> bluer took it your
> but bluest took it our
> away beyond where
>
> what a wonderful thing
> is the end of a string

(murmurs little you-i
as the hill becomes nil)
and will somebody tell
me why people let go

The ambidextrous compactness of the Joyce pun is one
of poetry's best weapons and is instinctive with E. E. Cummings, as where he tells how nonentity and "the general
menedgerr" "smokéd a robert burns cigerr to the god of
things like they err." The word "huge" in this book, and certain lines—for example, you "whose moving is more april
than the year"—remind one of earlier work by E. E. Cummings. If, however, one's individuality was not a mistake
from the first, it should not be a crime to maintain it; and
there are here poems that have a fortified expressiveness beyond any earlier best love poems. Like that painting in the
Cummings exhibition at the American-British Art Center
entitled "Paris Roofs, rue de la Bûcherie," Poem XXXIX,
containing the line "Swoop (shrill collective myth) into thy
grave," is as positive as a zebra and as tender as the new
moon.

This is the E. E. Cummings book of masterpieces. It will
provoke imitations, but mastery is inimitable—such as we
have in "the apples are (yes they're gravensteins)"; in "plato
told him:"; and in "what if a much of a which of a wind."
Indeed, in all the rest; for endeavoring to choose, there is
nothing to omit. Nothing? The reader who is so childish as
to hope that a book of wonders could be wonderful throughout will encounter obscenity and be disheartened. Obscenity
as a protest is better than obscenity as praise, but there is—
between the mechanics of power in a spark of feeling and
the mechanics of power in a speck of obscenity—an ocean

of difference, and it does not seem sagacious of either to mistake itself for the other. As for indignities—if one may ask admiration consciously to ignore and unconsciously to admire—this writing is an apex of positiveness and of indivisible, undismemberable joy. It is a thing of furious nuclear integrities; it need not argue with hate and fear, because it has annihilated them; "everybody never breathed quite so many kinds of yes)." When it appears to ask a question—

> i've come to ask you if there isn't a
> new moon outside your window saying if
> that's all, just if

—it has the answer to life's riddle. It is reiterating:

> death, as men call him, ends what they call men
> —but beauty is more now than dying's when

The paintings "have the purities of mushrooms blooming in darkness," says Mr. McBride, throwing light on the poetry's secret of beatitude, for poetry is a flowering and its truth is "a cry of a whole of a soul," not dogma; it is a positiveness that is joy, that we have in birdsongs and should have in ourselves; it is a "cry of alive with a trill like until" and is a poet's secret, "for his joy is more than joy." Defined by this book in what it says of life in general, "such is a poet and shall be and is."

THIS treatise *On the Making of Gardens*, first issued in England in 1909, is notable as an exposition of its subject and no less as a portrait of the impassioned mind—of its author as poet and moralist, "regarding his surroundings with analytic attention." Sir Francis Bacon's "Essay on Gardens" at last has a counterpart. Poetic implacability was never seen to better advantage than in the style of Sir George Sitwell, in which nicety is barbed with a kind of decorous ferocity, as when he says, "Forgery in art is not a crime unless it fails to deceive." Metaphor so merges with context as scarcely to be distinguishable from it—in the statement, say, that "architecture, the most useful of the arts, belongs to the passerby."

The glory of the book, however, is in its originality of emphasis—upon the Campagna ruins, for instance, lost at the horizon in a gleam of the sea, though "not like the sea, which is dreadful because it remembers not." "We must be ready," Sir George says, "to learn all that science can teach us concerning the laws of presentment." "When setting himself to anything," we are told in the Introduction by Sir Osbert Sitwell, the author's son, "no pain was spared, either to himself or to others." "He particularly liked to alter the levels at which full-grown trees were standing," Sir Osbert

[1] Review of Sir George Sitwell's *On the Making of Gardens*, in the *New York Times Book Review*, August 19, 1951.

says. "Two old yew trees in front of the dining-room windows at Renishaw were regularly heightened and lowered." Engineering zeal in any case is seen to have its verbal prototype. It is "the passion for ideality" which has excluded such words as "very" and "extremely" from these pages of consummate elegance. The secret of burnished writing is strong intention. The man is the style.

In garden-making the great secret of success, it would seem, is "the profound platitude that we should abandon the struggle to make nature beautiful round the house and should rather move the house to where nature is beautiful"; "the garden should be in sympathy with both . . . 'as if one were stepping from one room to another' "; and "like every other work of art, it should have a climax." It should be "presented with economy of the recipient's attention"— "without features which disturb or detract," since "if a picture be complete, everything that is added is something taken away."

The guiding principle of garden-makers of the Italian Renaissance, Sir George Sitwell says, was imagination. "We learn from them the value of contrast," and "if care has been taken to make the expectation less than the reality, we shall have the added thrill of wonder." At the Villa Mondragone, for instance, there is "a little iron balcony"; after "gloom and confinement as you step out upon it the boundless view takes your breath away." Inversely, while "all the landscape seems to swoon in a white haze of heat," one may have the contrast of unexpected shade in "the deep refreshing green of an avenue of cypresses half a millennium old."

In their mastery of "the water-art," Sir George likens the great Italians to "a sultan with his jewels or Turner playing with light," "prisoning the blue of the sea," "green of chrysoprase," or "the rainbow in a crystal spray." His imparting of technicalities is explicitness itself, as when he says, "The delicious softness of grass, gives at the first footstep a release from care, which should be proffered close to the house and if possible at a centre of beauty."

Sir George Sitwell shows us in this glittering treatise how to look at what we see; his stately observations are applicable to small as well as to great gardens; and throughout, an inescapable lesson is afforded us—that discipline results in freedom. "If the scheme has no air of permanence," we are told, "if it preaches the uncertainty of life and the uselessness of effort—the cup of beauty it offers will be tainted with sadness." "In a garden, a new character is put upon the individual. Instead of life's double face, every shadow is a friend."

"The garden is inimical to all evil passions; it stands for efficiency, for patience in labour, for strength in adversity, for the power to forgive." "In the garden of the Bamboo Grove, Buddha taught the conquest of self, and in the Garden of Sorrows, a greater teacher was found." Gardens are thus seen to be "a background for life"—"not for refreshment alone" but "for the unbending of a bow that it may shoot the stronger."

ANNA PAVLOVA [1]

"To enter the School of the Imperial Ballet is to enter a convent whence frivolity is banned, and where merciless discipline reigns," Pavlova tells us in the autobiographic miniature entitled *Pages of My Life*. In keeping with that statement was her ability to regard genius as a trust, concerning which vanity would be impossible. "My successes," she said, are "due to my ceaseless labour and to the merits of my teachers." And yet, whereas the impression of security she gave could have been the result of an exacting discipline, for there have been virtuosi whose dancing was flawless, she was compelling because of spiritual force that did not need to be mystery, she so affectionately informed her technique with poetry.

Something of this we see in the photograph of her taken at the age of twelve—in the erectness of the head; the absolutely horizontal brows indicating power of self-denial; eyes dense with imagination and sombered by solicitude; hair severely competent; the dress, dainty more than proud. "We were poor—very poor indeed, . . . my father having died two years after my birth," she says of childhood days with her mother in the country. "Bareheaded, and clad in an old cotton frock, I often would explore the woods close by the cottage. I enjoyed the mysterious aspect of the cloisterlike alleys under the fir trees," and "at times I wove myself a

[1] *Dance Index*, March 1944.

147

wreath of wildflowers and imagined myself to be the Beauty asleep in her enchanted castle."

Here are contrasts, romance unharmed by poverty and dreams that were ardor, recognizable in the very titles of parts danced in later years: the Butterfly, the Dragonfly, the Snowflake, Crystal Clear Spring, Fleur de Lys' Friend, Giselle "the newborn fairy, daughter of the breeze." And as the memoir tells further on, "In countries abroad, it was said there was 'something novel' in my dancing. Yet what I had done was merely to subordinate its physical elements to a psychological concept: over the matter-of-fact aspects of dancing—that is, dancing *per se*—I have attempted to throw a spiritual veil of poetry. . . ." So above all, it is affection for beauty that is unmistakable—reverie which was reverence. At even her "first motion," wrote René Jean, "she seems about to embrace the whole world"; world being a term precise in more than the immediate sense, for in her dancing with persons, remoteness marked her every attitude. It is the uncontaminated innocence of her fervor that is really her portrait in the pose in which she is protectingly entwined with an actual swan—guarding and adoring what is almost a menace. Again the paradox of spirit contradictory with fact, in the *Autumn Bacchanal*—her fingers resting as a leaf might have come to rest; and as the Dragonfly, she inclines the point of the left wing toward her head by the merest incurving touch of the fingers from below, as if there were on it silver-dust or dew that must not be disturbed, while controlling the right wing by curving it over the wrist, with thumb and finger meeting upon the firmly held edge, though just within it. These truthful hands, the most sincere, the least greedy imaginable, are indeed "like

priests, a sacerdotal gravity impressed upon their features";
yet, as noticed by Cyril Beaumont, they "were a little large
for her arms, and the fingers inclined to be thick"; so the
illusion of grace, though not accidental, must have been a
concomitant of her subconscious fire; her expression, Mr.
Beaumont continues, being as "changeable as the very face
of nature; her body responding to the mood of a dance as a
tuning-fork vibrates to a blow." And in the fervent reminiscences of her by Victor Dandré, her husband, we find that,
losing patience with the lack of individuality in her dancers,
she would say to them, "Why do you go about expressing
nothing? Cry when you want to cry and laugh when you
want to laugh."

Her feet, remarkable for the power of the ankle, their
high arch, and "toes of steel," made her *pizzicati* on tiptoe
and steadily held pauses possible; but not easy, as noted by
Mr. Dandré, since her long main toe, by which the whole
weight of her body had to be borne, did not provide the
squared support of the more level toes of the somewhat
typically thickset virtuoso. Yet "when standing on one toe,
she could change her entire balance," André Olivéroff says,
"by moving the muscles of her instep. This may seem a
small thing, but it was one of the many that contributed to
her dancing the perpetual slight novelty that made it impossible for an instant to tire of watching her."

Theodore Stier, musical director of her performances for
sixteen years, says, "She is, I think, the most sincere woman
it ever has been my good fortune to meet, sincere with herself as with others"; and this doubly undeceived honesty was
matched by logic. She did not admire Degas, because he had
delineated attitudes not movement; and when inventing

three social dances—the Pavlovana, the Gavotte Renaissance (not to be confused with the *Gavotte Pavlova*), and
the Czarina Waltz—she took precaution that every step
and pose should be within the ability of the average dancer.
Her utter straightness of spirit was matched by an incapacity
for subterfuge that is all but spectacular; as when in speaking of stage fright she admitted that each time before an
appearance she was subject to it, and "this emotion," she
said, "instead of decreasing with time, becomes stronger and
stronger. For I am increasingly conscious of . . . my re-
sponsibilities."

"Her feet are light as wings, her rhythm speaks of
dreams," has been said by many in many ways; but if
dreams are to transform us, there must be power behind
them, and in Pavlova the unself-sparing dynamo, will power,
by which she was to be incommoded and to incommode
others, made itself felt when she was not more than eight.
To celebrate Christmas, she was—for the first time—on her
way to the Maryinsky Theatre with her mother, and, in-
quiring what they were to see, was told, "You are going to
enter fairyland." "When we left the theatre," she says, "I
was living in a dream. I kept thinking of the day when I
should make my first appearance on the stage, in the part of
the Sleeping Beauty." Begging to be allowed to enter the
School of the Imperial Ballet, and refused by her mother, she
then says, "It was only a few days later, wondering at my firmness of purpose, that she complied with my desire and took
me to see the Director of the School." Deferred by him until
she was ten, since no child might be admitted earlier, she
persevered after two years in persuading her mother to request admittance again, and was accepted. However tiring a

journey might have been, "it was rare for her to go to her hotel in a town where she was to appear, before visiting the theatre," Mr. Stier says, and in the draftiness of a darkened stage, she would practice while others rested. At rehearsal she was a "relentless taskmaster," we are told. Mr. Dandré says, "She was firm because she knew she was right." The word "firm" again;

ANNA PAVLOVA

THE INCOMPARABLE

PRIMA BALLERINA ASSOLUTA

stamped in violet on the back of one of her St. Petersburg photographs, is, one feels, part of the likeness.

Will power has its less noble concomitant, willfulness, and although Pavlova could not be convinced on occasion, that she was mistaken in giving aid to an impostor she pitied, or that she should desist from an over-impetuosity that she might repent of, she "did not know the meaning of the word cynicism." "Better thrice imposed on," she said, "than turn the empty away; . . . it is so easy to forgive people who must find it hard to forgive themselves." Willful and will-powerful though she was, however, a modest deference of attitude was so natural to her that it marked her as all but one with the snowdrops and wildflowers she loved. Ever accurate, when wishing to make clear that the term ballerina is not used in speaking of a dancer who is merely one of the ballet, she uses the passive voice: "I left the Ballet School at the age of sixteen and shortly afterwards was permitted to style myself Première Danseuse, which is an official title. . . . Later I was granted the title Ballerina, which but four other dancers of the present time have received." Here again, a persuasion of contrasts: undogmatic decisiveness, strength of foot with lightness of body; technical proficiency with poetic feeling; aloofness and simplicity in one who had chosen as her art that most exposed form of self-expression, dancing. It is said that "she proceeded intelligently, calmly, prudently," and that as she stood on tiptoe, the sole of her foot was "an absolute vertical"—a proof of "adequate training." Yet with the focused power there was an elfin quality of suddenness as incalculable as the fire in a prism, suggested by the darting descent to one knee, in *The Dragonfly*. "When she was excited about anything," André Olivéroff says, "she had a way of clenching her hand and pressing it to her mouth, glancing sideways as though in search of a possible adventure." May not this propensity to bewitchment explain the fact that she found irksome some of the portraits of her that others admire? and that she would try, as she entered the theater, not to see her simulacrum, flaunted to attract patronage? Nothing is so striking as the disparity between her many likenesses; and nothing so eludes portraiture as ecstasy.

In dancing we have the rhythms of music made visible; also color and design; and if the result is to be more than acrobacy, power of dramatic expression. Pavlova was virtuoso of each: of slender form and aerial buoyancy, with strength of foot, perfect technique, which it was ever her study to "repair," and interpretive power whereby she "acted the dancing and danced the acting."

Through its harmonized symmetries, style combines "the ability to disengage and coordinate elements"; and in her attitudes, as in the timing of steps, Pavlova possessed it. She was balanced harmony, in her thinking and in her motions. Having begun the brief account of her life with the forest, she concluded with it: "The wind rustles through the branches of the fir trees in the forest opposite my veranda, the forest through which as a child I longed to rove. The stars shine in the evening gloom. I have come to the end of these few recollections."

So with pictorial symmetry. In the photograph taken at Ivy House, of her seated on the grass beside the chair of Maestro Cecchetti, her teacher of dancing, the descending line of the propped forearm, of her dress and other hand, of ankle and foot, continues to the grass with the naturalness of a streamer of seaweed—a stately serpentine which imparts to the seated figure the ease of a standing one. Again, in the photograph in which she is seated on the wide steps of a building in Italy—her hands on her sunshade which rests on her lap—the middle finger and little finger of each hand, higher than the finger between, adhere to classic formula but with the spontaneous curve of the iris petal.

It seems to have been an idiosyncrasy of Pavlova's that one hand should copy rather than match the other, as in the Aimé Stevens portrait, in which the hands, holding a string of jade and lifted as though to feel the rain, tend both in the same direction, from left to right (Pavlova's right), instead of diverging equilaterally with the oppositeness of horns. In *Spring Flowers*, the right foot turning left is imitated by the left foot's half-moon curve to the left. *Giselle* —hands reaching forward, feet (tiptoe) in lyrelike verticals —is all of a piece. Everything moves together, like a fish leaping a weir; the tiny butterfly wings seen in silhouette, weighting the space above the level skirt that in soaring out repeats the airy horizontal of the arms. And as with the swan curves of *Giselle*, so with the perfectly consolidated verticals in the *Gavotte*, *The Dragonfly*, and *The Swan*. Balance is master.

Harmony of design would be lacking were it not for what does not show—the devoted effort that made it possible. "The Dancer," Pavlova said, "must practise her exercises every day." She must "feel so at ease so far as technique is concerned, that when on the stage she need devote to it not a thought and may concentrate upon expression, upon the feelings which must give life to the dances she is performing."

Observers said, "It is as though some internal power impels the arabesque"; "even when engaged in extreme feats of virtuosity and bravura, she preserves spontaneity and ease." "I was essentially a lyric dancer," she says—in the Provençal sense of a dance as a song, a *ballada*. She did not make the Italian mistake of introducing school exercises in her dancing and "never was interested in purposeless virtuosity"; would not, had she been able, have cared to be a circus virtuoso, suspended by teeth and wrist, revolving in a blur for half an hour. "When she danced," Mr. Beaumont says, "the hands seemed delicate and the fingers tapering. . . . She turned pirouettes with an elegant ease, and though she rarely did more than two or three, she executed them with such a brio that they had the effect of half-a-dozen."

"The stage is like a magnifying glass. Everything tends toward exaggeration," and as in music sensibility does not misuse the pedal, so with Pavlova; humor, esprit, a sense of style—and also a moral quality—made it impossible for her to show off, to be hard, to be dull; the same thing that in life made her self-controlled rather than a prison to what she prized. "Her dancing," says Mr. Beaumont, quoting "a French writer," was " '*la danse de toujours, dansée comme jamais*'—the dance of everyday as never dansed before"; and speaking of the "Gavotte danced to 'The Glowworm' music, by Paul Lincke, nothing could be more ordinary from the viewpoint of both choreography and music, yet she made it into a delicious miniature of the Merveilleuse period."

Although rhythm is the repetition of a sound or effect at regulated intervals, independence of rhythm is essential, and Pavlova never contented herself with literalities; her inventions—the trill on tiptoe, the long pause on tiptoe, and the impulsive pirouette—being temperament's enlarging of accepted convention. "Her hands possess a life of their own," it was said. In the little finger apart from the fourth, one deduces independence; in its double curve, poetic feeling; in the slightly squared fingertips, originality—qualities which seem to have something in common with a similar freedom in the dancing of Nijinsky, and with the stateliness of Greta Garbo. One recalls, moreover, in connection with the independent fingers, Pavlova's choosing to appear at the Palace Theatre in London and at the Hippodrome in New York. She indeed was, as has been remarked by someone, "a teaching."

A special aspect of her independence was what Lincoln Kirstein calls the "openness" of her dancing, as in the Gavotte she advanced with the swirling grace of a flag. Mr. Olivéroff says, "I have sometimes felt that I would rather see her walk out on the stage to take a curtain call than see her dance *Swan* or *Papillon*"; throwing light on her own statement, "Whatever a person does or refrains from doing out of fear, is bad." Moreover, Mr. Beaumont says, "As the microphone amplifies the slightest sound, so her least movement held the attention of the audience," and we can understand how "she was never so successful in her ballets as in her *soli* and *pas de deux*"; how "the ballet, being a composite work, . . . fell apart with Pavlova and her partner executing *soli* or *pas de deux*; the others coming on at intervals when it was necessary for the principals to rest."

Fairyland! It may be ecstasy but it is a land of pathos, and although Pavlova's parts were poetry, they were in most instances symbols of grief: Giselle, a Wili of the moonlight who must at dawn return underground from the world of light and love; La Péri, Servant of the Pure, who "realized that yon flower of life (the scarlet lotus) was not for her"; Crystal Clear Spring, the Ghost King's daughter, who warns her sisters not to open the door to the stranger, that if they disobey they must die, then chooses to die with them; Esmeralda, the forsaken gipsy who must dance at the festivities in honor of her betrayer; the Dying Rose, the Swan.

Does imagination care to look upon a sculptured fairy, a live or any demonstrable creature of the moonlight? What could constitute a greater threat to illusion than the impersonated quiver of a dragonfly, or be less like a swan than two little wings arising unbiologically from the waist? It would seem that Pavlova was obliged to overcome her roles, and for the most part her costumes, for which she needed an Omar Kiam with a sense of structural continuity, and novelty that does without novelty; though one must make an exception: the Gavotte, as portrayed in Malvina Hoffman's wax statuette. Mordkin's gladiator-like torso might

identify itself with his roles, whereas Pavlova was, theoretically, always at a disadvantage. Is the motion-picture of her
Death of the Swan entirely becoming to her? Photographs
of her dances taken even at the good moment fail, one feels,
of the effect she had in life; and "those who never saw her
dance may ask what she did that made her so wonderful. It
is not so much what she did," Mr. Beaumont says, "as how
she did it"; and one suspects that she so intently thought
the illusion she wished to create that it made her illusive—
hands and feet obeying imagination in a way that compensated for any flaw. She had power, moreover, for a most unusual reason—she did not project as valuable the personality
from which she could not escape. Of her Dying Swan, Mr.
Beaumont says, "The emotion transferred was so overpowering that it seemed a mockery to applaud when the
dance came to an end." This impression is corroborated by
others; Andrei Levensohn's summary of that dance (the
translation is here slightly altered) being a lament as well as
a description: "Arms folded, on tiptoe, she dreamily and
slowly circles the stage. By even, gliding motions of the
hands, returning to the background whence she emerged,
she seems to strive toward the horizon, as though a moment
more and she will fly—exploring the confines of space with
her soul. The tension gradually relaxes and she sinks to
earth, arms moving faintly as in pain. Then faltering with
irregular steps toward the edge of the stage—leg bones
a-quiver like the strings of a harp—by one swift forward-
gliding motion of the right foot to earth, she sinks on the
left knee—the aerial creature struggling against earthly
bonds, and there, transfixed by pain, she dies."

"I imagined," she said, ". . . I dreamed that I was a

Ballerina and spent my whole life dancing, like a butterfly";
but her dance of the swan was a rite—arms folded crusader-
like, in the sign of the cross—"the rhythms disintegrating"
symbolically, as in Giselle's dancing they disintegrated under madness, literally undoing her earthly joy. "Pavlova was
simple, simple as a child is simple," André Olivéroff says,
"and yet there was a great tenderness about her, sadder than
a child's and more peaceful." Why should one so innocent,
so natural, so ardent, be sad? If "self-control is the essential
condition of conveying emotion," and giving is giving up,
we still cannot feel that renunciation had made Pavlova sad;
may it have been that for lives that one loves there are things
that even love cannot do?

Of herself as she stood on the balcony of her hotel in
Stockholm she said, "I bowed from time to time; and sud-
denly they began to sing. . . . I sought vainly for a way of expressing my gratitude. But even after I had thrown my roses
and lilies and violets and lilacs to them they seemed loath to
withdraw." And "in Belgium, following a brief season in
Liége," as recalled by Mr. Stier, "when we went to settle
with the various newspapers in which the performances had
been advertised, to our astonishment, they refused to accept
payment. Pavlova has done so much for the national appre-
ciation of art, they explained, that we cannot bring ourselves
to accept money from her."

"How rare it is," she said to André Olivéroff, "to find an
artist who combines passion with intellect, who dances always with a mind and body both trained, and with a heart
that is on fire. Of the two, if I had to say, I would always
choose the heart. But that alone is not enough. You must
have both." In giving happiness, she truly "had created

her crown of glory and placed it upon her brows." That which is able to change the heart proves itself.

PARTIAL CHRONOLOGY

Anna (Matveyevna) Pavlova was born February 16, 1882, in St. Petersburg, but her name day was January 30th.

She made her debut at the Maryinsky Theatre, January 1, 1899, and became Prima Ballerina in 1901.

In 1907, with Adolph Bolm as partner, she went on tour with a company—Helsingfors, Stockholm, Copenhagen, Prague, Berlin.

In 1909 she danced in two performances with the Diaghilev Company during their Paris season at the Châtelet Theatre; also that same season, crossed to London, to dance at a party given by Lady Londesborough in honor of King Edward VII and Queen Alexandra.

In 1910, April 18, she made her debut in London at the Palace Theatre, and in that year visited the United States—also Canada—on a tour beginning in New York, where she danced at the Metropolitan Opera House.

In 1910 she purchased Ivy House, North East Road, Hampstead, just outside London.

In 1911 she returned to the Palace Theatre, bringing *La Nuit*, *Papillon*, and various ballets.

In 1912, 1913, 1914, she returned to London. "Jealousies, desertions, unpunctualities and demands for leaves of absence on the part of her Russian dancers made it necessary to replace certain of them, until finally the entire ballet was British. Then," says Theodore Stier, "began an era of peace for Pavlova such as she had not thought possible."

From 1914 onward she made extended tours over the world.

In 1920 an Orphan Home for twenty refugee children from Russia was founded by her, in the rue Chemin de Fer, Paris. This was her fondest charity and in preference to receiving a birthday gift it became her custom to request of her company that they give to her for her orphans what might have been contributed toward a gift for herself.

In January 1931 she died in Holland, of pleurisy. While en route to the Hague via the Riviera, to begin a tour, after a sleepless night in a train that had stood on a siding all night, she caught cold—recorded thus reverently by Mr. Beaumont: "Hardly settled in the Hotel des Indes, she fell ill; the flame that was her life, flickered, burnt low, and half an hour after midnight, on Friday, January 23rd, went out."

INDEX

INDEX